Praise for the
Angie Amalfi Mysteries

"...the humor, the wit and the satisfying twists of this romantic tale...
just the right measures of intrigue, danger, jealousy and warmth."
—*The Time Machine*

"A tasty treat for all mystery and suspense lovers who like food for
thought, murder and a stab at romance."
—*The Armchair Detective*

"Joanne Pence is a master chef."
—*Mystery Scene*

"Singularly unusual c'
—*The Mystery*

"Pence can satisfy th   mystery
reader."
—*Literary Tin.*

"Angie Amalfi is the queen of the culinary sleuths."
—*RT Book Club*

"A winner...Angie is a character unlike any other in the genre."
—*Santa Rosa Press Democrat*

"A wicked flair for light humor...a delightful reading concoction."
—*Gothic Journal*

"Another terrific book...a bit of Lucille Ball and the Streets of San
Francisco"
—*Tales From a Red Herring*

"Murder couldn't be served up in a more delicious manner."
—*The Paperback Forum*

Cook's Big Day

An Angie Amalfi Mystery

JOANNE PENCE

QUAIL HILL PUBLISHING

Quail Hill Publishing
PO Box 64
Eagle, ID 83616

Visit our website at www.quailhillpublishing.net

First Quail Hill Publishing Paperback Printing: September 2015
First Quail Hill E-book: September 2015

ISBN-13: 978-0692529782

ISBN-10: 0692529780

To my readers

Cook's Big Day

Chapter 1

Monday, 1 p.m. - 5 days, 2 hours before the wedding

Angelina Amalfi felt as if she were walking on air as she entered the ballroom of La Belle Maison, the premier wedding reception location in San Francisco. Once a mansion located partway up the northeast slope of Telegraph Hill, the home had been renovated some years earlier into an events venue. While the main floor held an elegant reception area with sofas and arms chairs, a commercial kitchen, and staff offices, the entire upper floor had been converted into a large, opulent ballroom with crystal chandeliers and gold sconces.

Picture windows faced north and east, commanding a view of San Francisco Bay from Alcatraz Island to the Bay Bridge. White-cloth covered tables circled the dance floor.

It was Monday afternoon, and that coming Saturday Angie's long-awaited wedding would take place—the date that she and everyone who knew her had come to think of as her Big Day.

With Angie was Sally Lankowitz, La Belle Maison's events coordinator. She had the privilege—her word—to see to it that the wedding reception went exactly the way Angie hoped it would, from the meal to the placement of the wedding cake, to the band, the music, the dancing, the photographers, and the timing of each important step along the way. She was a pleasant woman with over-sized red-framed glasses that perched on a stubby nose and covered a round, ruddy-cheeked face. Her brown hair was short and curly, and she wore a simple cotton print dress with sensibly short, squat heels. And no wedding ring.

Angie had toured the facility and met with Sally a few months earlier when she first contracted with La Belle Maison to hold her wedding reception. But now everything felt more *real,* as if it were actually going to happen. Her Big Day was unimaginably close.

"This room is going to look simply beautiful," Sally gushed, holding her arms out, hands raised as she walked to the center of the large space and turned all the way around. Angie's eyes followed where Sally's hands led. "I do love the soft rose color you chose. It's so feminine, it will make you stand out even more with your dark hair and snow white dress. You'll be like a china doll."

"Thank you." Angie guessed that was a compliment. She was short, only five-two, and being likened to any kind of "doll" didn't sit well.

"Now," Sally said, with a momentary clasping of her hands, "let's talk about your wedding cake. I'm sure it will be gorgeous, so I suggest that you—"

"There you are!" A woman's harsh, shrill voice called.

Angie turned to see a young woman storming towards them. She was tall, with long, wavy blond hair, and wore a tight black suit with a short skirt. The heels on her black shoes were at least four-inches high.

Angie stood a little straighter.

"Oh, Ms. Redmun," Sally said. She didn't sound happy. "I don't believe we have an appointment."

"I don't need an appointment for this. I only have a couple of quick issues." Ms. Redmun flicked a lock of highlighted dirty blonde hair off her brow as she glanced at Angie. She was attractive and appeared to be in her mid-to-late twenties. "Do you work here as well?"

"No," Angie said. "My wedding reception will be held here Saturday."

"Oh. Nice." Her tone was dismissive. "My *entire* wedding will be held here Wednesday evening. An evening soiree will allow us to use the deck as long as Ms. Officious here"—she waggled her thumb at Sally—"can understand my simple request."

Sally looked taken aback. "Excuse me—"

"Wednesday?" Angie asked. "Your wedding is on a Wednesday?"

"Yes, because—"

Sally interrupted. "Let me introduce the two of you. Angie Amalfi, Taylor Redmun. Now, Taylor, I'll be done with Angie in just a little while. She does, after all, have an appointment. If you'd like to wait in the *waiting* room, Laurie will get you some coffee." Angie's antennae rose even higher. Sally had always been all but cloyingly courteous to her.

"No need. I'll just wait here." Taylor folded her arms and glared at them both.

Sally again faced Angie. "As I was saying, you probably want to have your cake on the north side of the room. From the windows, there's a beautiful view of the bay, which makes a lovely backdrop for photos of the cake cutting ceremony."

"I see," Angie murmured. She wanted to pinch herself that soon she would actually be the bride cutting a wedding cake.

"That sounds lovely."

"I'm having mine put on the south wall," Taylor loudly announced. "How good can any photos be with glare from the windows ruining everything? I've learned from my camera people in Hollywood that that's a no-no. I mean, really."

Her words caught Sally's attention. "I don't believe we have the furniture set-up for your wedding marked that way."

"I know." Taylor strolled closer to Sally, hands on hips. She abruptly turned her back on the events coordinator and perused the room but continued to speak. "It's one of the few little things I wanted to tell you. In fact, I have no idea why any bride would want to have her cake on the north wall. The more I thought about it, the more I knew you were wrong to suggest it."

Sally's cheeks turned red. "I see, well, we'll discuss it later." As she glanced at Angie, her brown eyes seemed smaller than ever behind her large eyeglass frames. "Now, Angie, where were we? The cake, there, by the windows?"

"Well," Angie murmured. "Maybe by that south wall is a better idea."

"The glare is slight, and has never been a problem, I assure you. The south side of the room has the staircase. The cake makes a much better presentation as the guests come up the stairs if it's at the opposite end of the space," Sally said, her voice getting higher with each word.

"What's more important?" Taylor asked. "A moment's presentation or a lifetime of great photographs? Also, I want my DJ to be on the west wall. No sense him being on the east and blocking the view from the windows."

"But the plumbing for the ice machine and refrigeration for

the wet bar are on the west wall," Sally said.

"Don't be ridiculous." Taylor all but sneered at Sally. "I'd like the wet bar on the east wall, and my DJ, who will be playing my *personal* playlist, over there on the west."

Sally looked increasingly distraught. "The wires for the speakers are on the east wall."

"I wonder if I want my band in front of the windows," Angie murmured.

Sally twirled her way. "But as I was saying, the wires—"

Taylor glared at her, lips pursed. "For crying out loud. Bar on east, DJ on the west, cake on the south. Sheesh." She tucked a lock of hair behind her ear. Her hair was thick, long and stylishly wavy, falling well below her shoulders. "It's hardly brain surgery!"

"I wonder if that would work out better," Angie said, fingers to chin.

Sally, her face pinched and tight, turned to Angie. "Only if you want your wet bar to have no ice or refrigeration, the wires for the speakers going across the middle of the dance floor, and your cake shoved in a space where people entering the reception are milling around and it will hardly be seen."

"I don't have a band!" Taylor harrumphed. "You know that!"

"I was talking to Miss Amalfi." Sally sounded more desperate with each word.

"Why would you be talking to *her?*" Taylor cocked an eyebrow. "I'm telling you what I want for my reception, and she's just standing there looking like a potted plant."

"A potted plant?" Angie gasped. "I'm the one with the appointment! Who do you think you are, taking over my reception planning?"

"Well, for one thing, you've got a whole week. I only have two days, and this so-called wedding 'assistant' has been anything but helpful. I have to do all the thinking myself."

"I'm sorry, Taylor." Sally looked on the verge of tears. "I'm trying to help you, but you keep making changes."

"I do not make changes on a whim. I come up with enhancements—to do the job, in other words, that you aren't capable of doing!"

Sally gaped, speechless, tears welling in her eyes.

Angie spun towards Taylor. "Will you *please* butt out? You're doing nothing but upsetting Sally, confusing me, and mucking up this entire process."

Taylor loomed over her. "Why are you so pushy? I've only got a couple of changes and then I'm out of here!"

Angie put her hands on her hips. "I'm pushy? I don't think so. If you'd kept your bossy-pants mouth shut, I would have been finished by now."

"Bossy-pants? What kind of infantile word is that?"

"If you prefer a more adult word that starts with a 'b,' I'll certainly use it," Angie said.

"Sally, I demand you do something about this creature," Taylor said. "I'm an important person. I don't have time for this."

Angie was not a violent person, but it was all she could do not to slap the woman. "Important in your own mind, maybe. But sure as hell not in anyone else's."

Taylor raised her chin. "I'll have you know, I'm going to be in a movie."

"What movie? *Bridezilla?*"

"Why you little slut!"

"Stop!" Sally screamed. "I can't take it anymore! I can't take the orders, the bickering, the mind changing, the disappointment. The fact that not one of you ever thinks about me." She burst into tears. "I'm here trying to help, and all I get is criticism. You make me sick. Every last one of you."

With that, she turned and ran from the room, leaving Angie and Taylor both slack-jawed in the large empty space.

He looked at the bride and smiled. His bride.

She was beautiful, and everything a bride should be. She wore a white dress with seed pearls and lace, a white veil over her face. White satin shoes, white elbow-length gloves.

Perfect.

She lay on her back on the bed, and he lifted the veil off her face just as he would have done on their wedding day. He leaned near and pressed his lips to hers, then lightly ran his hand over her neck, her shoulders, and along the front of her dress to her small waist. He loved her; he wanted her.

He took hold of the hem of her dress and slid his hand under it along her calf, moving upward. But then he stopped and stood up straight.

He didn't care for the bright red lipstick she was wearing. He found a tissue and wiped it off, then looked over the lipstick shades in the knapsack he carried and found a soft pink. Carefully, he covered her full lips with color. Much better. Kissable.

At the thought, he bent forward and kissed her again, much longer this time. He only wished her mouth under his was soft instead of hard and dry; warm instead of cold. But none of that mattered. He crawled onto the bed beside her, circled her with his arms, and slid his fingers under the neckline of the dress, just below her collarbone, then inched lower.

He heard a noise and stopped.

He was in a storeroom in the basement of an old, run-down apartment building. The room had been filled with ugly furniture abandoned years before. He moved it all out when he moved his bride in. He also brought in their matrimonial bed, a chair and a lamp. The only window, high on the wall, was at street level when viewed from the outside. It was small, awning-style, and opened by turning the latch and pulling it inward. He had painted it black and nailed it shut. But now, someone was pushing it open.

He froze.

Two teenage boys peered through the window and met his eyes. Their mouths dropped open in shock, but their shock turned to horror as they took in the scene before them. With shrieks and cries, they backed away and ran.

He jumped off the bed. "Wait!" he yelled as he climbed onto the chair to look out the window. "Come back here!"

But the boys were gone.

Chapter 2

Wednesday nights were usually quiet in Homicide, so even though San Francisco Homicide Inspector Rebecca Mayfield and her partner, Inspector Bill Sutter, were the on-call detectives that week, she had gone home early.

Now, she sat in her two-room apartment in her pajamas, a bowl of popcorn on her lap, and her ten-pound Chinese Crested Hairless/Chihuahua mix at her side. She was shedding tears over a weepy old romance from Netflix when her cell phone began to buzz.

Homicide's dispatcher gave her an address.

She dried her eyes and went into the bedroom to get dressed. The last thing she wanted to do was to look at a dead body, but it was her job. Thirty minutes later she wended her way up the narrow, twisting roads of Telegraph Hill. Police cars told her she had reached the crime scene, but she was surprised by the location, nonetheless.

The two-story building looked as if it had once been a large, luxurious home, but now a discrete chiseled stone plaque near the door read "La Belle Maison."

As Rebecca showed her credentials to the uniformed SFPD officer guarding the front door, another officer approached. "Inspector Mayfield?" he asked.

At her nod, he gave his name, Carl Beamer, and explained that he and his partner were first on the scene after 9-1-1 reported a number of calls from a party at the location.

Rebecca entered the ornate establishment with Officer Beamer. "The victim's up there," Beamer said, pointing to the wide-curving staircase to the left of the foyer. "We stopped everyone from leaving and moved them into the living room, or whatever it is, to clear the crime scene. They want to go home and are getting pretty upset."

She nodded and glanced in the direction Beamer indicated, to a room with a marble fireplace, sofas and chairs, and a several pockets of nicely dressed people huddled together.

The way they glared at her, upset wasn't the word she'd have used. Ready to riot was more likely.

Near her was a coat and hat check area, and beyond it, a hallway.

"Down the hall," Beamer said, "are some offices. We put the victim's family in there for privacy."

She nodded, and decided to take a quick walk through the ground floor before going up to see the body. Rebecca had learned that was a good operating practice. She had seen a few situations where a homicide cop made a bonehead assumption about a crime, and even destroyed some potential evidence, simply because he hadn't taken a moment to look over the location beyond the exact spot where the body was found.

Where a dining room most likely once stood, large, well-appointed men's and women's restrooms had been built, and beyond them was a small service elevator.

Last of all, she entered the kitchen, a stainless steel wonderland of appliances, from enormous Sub-zero refrigerators, to commercial grade stoves. It had large, deep sinks, stainless steel countertops, pots, pans, bowls, and enough cutting implements to make a knife thrower in a circus happy. A door led from the kitchen to an enclosed porch, and then out to a back alley lined with garbage cans and a dumpster.

"Time to head upstairs," she said to Beamer.

Reaching the ballroom, she saw a cluster of police to one side near the back, and assumed that was the location of the victim. In the center, looking rather lonely in the large space, Rebecca counted four round tables with six place settings at each, and a dance floor. The decorations were white, with white flowers and white bells. They gave her a bad feeling about just what kind of a "party" this might have been.

On one wall, a portable bar had been set up, and on the opposite wall, a station for a DJ.

As she approached the cluster of police officers, they stepped aside so she could see the victim.

She gasped.

Not only had no one told her the party was a wedding reception, no one had said that the victim was the bride.

The bride lay sprawled atop the table, face down in the wedding cake. The table was oblong, the cake in the middle. She looked as if she had stood at one end of the table and toppled forward onto the cake. Her feet dangled in the air.

Blood, lots of blood, oozed from a chef's knife protruding from her back. Blood saturated her dress, the table cloth, and dripped onto the floor.

"Oh, my," Rebecca gasped. She had seen plenty of dead bodies, but something about the bride got to her. "Her name?"

"Taylor Redmun," Beamer replied. "Or, I guess, Taylor

Redmun-Blythe since the wedding ceremony had taken place before this happened."

Rebecca nodded. "We must have over twenty witnesses. Has anyone stepped forward? Are they saying who did this?"

"It's hard to believe, but all we've heard is that no one saw anything other than the fact that the bride came through those swinging doors." He pointed to doors not far from the wedding cake. "Apparently they open to a small room where the caterer can stage the food he brings up on the elevator, keep extras of anything he might need, or whatever. The service elevator is at the back of the space. Anyway, the guests said the bride burst out of there, through the swinging doors, then ran and stumbled towards the cake with her arms out as if she wanted to grab it, but instead, she fell on it. That was when they saw the knife...and the blood."

"Who saw it?"

"It sounds like all of them. Apparently, everyone went crazy, screaming, and running for the exits. The wedding planner, Sally Lankowitz, somehow managed to keep her wits, and she told everyone to sit down and that they couldn't leave until the police arrived."

"Where is she now?"

"In her office. She's quite shaken up, as you can imagine. Officer Donaldson is with her."

"Where's the groom?"

"He's in the owner's office with some of his close friends and relatives."

"Name?"

"Leland Blythe."

"And the bride's relatives?"

"I don't know. No one came forward."

Rebecca saw that the victim had been an attractive woman, very slim, probably around 5'8", with long, thick blonde hair. She wore a wedding ring with a substantial diamond, and her dress had intricate beading that probably cost a pretty penny.

"Did anyone say why she had left the ballroom to go into the anteroom?" Rebecca asked.

Beamer looked at the other officers. All shook their heads. "Guess not," he said. "I heard some speculation that she might have used the elevator to come back upstairs from the woman's bathroom, although most people used the stairs. Nobody knows for sure."

Rebecca was about to ask where the deceased's belongings were—her handbag, phone, wallet—when the Crime Scene Unit showed up. The photographer immediately began taking photos and recording the scene.

Shortly after them, Evelyn Ramirez, the medical examiner, entered with her assistants. "One of these days I'm going to arrive before you do," she said to Rebecca as she snapped latex gloves into place. "But I see I've beaten Bill Sutter, as usual."

"And where's the challenge in that?" Rebecca asked with a wry smile. She and Ramirez were accustomed to showing up at crime scenes long before Rebecca's thinking-about-retirement partner. She wished he would turn in his retirement papers and get it over with instead of spending almost every waking hour pondering and talking about it. Ironically, he was still a good detective when he put his mind to it.

The M.E. leaned over the deceased to get a better look at her. When the photographer gave the okay, she rolled the victim to one side, and then the other. The knife wound was the only evident cause of death thus far.

"It doesn't appear as if there'll be any surprises here," Ramirez said, straightening. "It's unlikely anything other than the chef's knife is the murder weapon. Given the size of the blade, it may have penetrated her lungs or caused some other horrific internal bleeding. With either injury, she could potentially walk a few feet before collapsing."

"How soon will you be able to do an autopsy on her?" Rebecca asked.

"Tomorrow morning."

"Thanks," Rebecca said.

She went into the anteroom. It held an empty table, and a set of shelves lined with a number of sets of salt and pepper shakers, sugar bowls, powdered creamers, clean cutlery, dessert plates, and carving knives. A rolling cart with dirty plates, knives, forks, and spoons had been haphazardly shoved to one side of the room.

She saw no blood, but it's possible the bridal gown absorbed most of it as the bride fled from her killer.

Rebecca left the anteroom to head downstairs to interview the guests and the wedding party, leaving the M.E. and CSI to do their jobs.

Chapter 3

"Oh, no!" Angie collapsed onto the sofa in the living room of her penthouse apartment high atop San Francisco's Russian Hill. A tragedy had struck.

She had spent the day packing the apartment for her big move across town to the home she would share with her fiancé, Homicide Inspector Paavo Smith, and had even turned down seeing Paavo that evening because she felt too hot, sweaty, and dusty. How had she accumulated so much junk? She had a pile of donations for St. Vincent de Paul to pick up, and a much larger pile of boxes of things to take with her.

But when she pulled a pale green sweater from the closet and put it in the donation bag, deciding she never did like the color, thoughts of her wedding washed over her and she realized that something was *less than perfect*.

That, more than weariness, caused her collapse.

How could anything so heinous happen? She had spent the last five months meticulously planning every exciting, joy-filled detail of her Big Day, such as when to do her hair and make-up; when to put on her wedding dress; what to use to decorate the pews in the church; what to use to decorate the car she and Paavo as well as her family would ride in; how to decorate party favors for the guests; the size of candles on the tables; even the timing of her departure with her husband—*husband*, such a beautiful word!—to their tower suite at the Fairmont Hotel where they would spend the night before leaving on their Hawaiian honeymoon.

She had thought about and planned her wedding day for so long that the possibility of anything being *less than perfect* was simply unacceptable. She had lain awake at night going over lists. She had lists of everything she needed to do, plus what everyone else involved with her Big Day needed to do. She even had lists of lists.

The difficulty was that not only did she want everything to be perfect, but also different. As part of a large Italian family, she'd been to many, many weddings. Plus, all four of her older sisters had had their own "special" weddings. She didn't want just another run-of-the-mill wedding that would blend into the stew of family get-togethers. Her wedding day, somehow, needed to stand out from the crowd.

The wedding ceremony itself would hold no surprises. It would take place in the church her family attended when she was growing up—the church where her parents and sisters had gotten married, Saints Peter and Paul, in San Francisco's North Beach district.

That meant she had to concentrate on the reception.

A monumental struggle ensued to get the owner of La Belle Maison to add her to his reception calendar in something less than the sixteen months most people had to wait. Finally, desperate, she had called her cousin Richie, who seemed to know his way around the city and its movers-and-shakers better than anyone else she could think of. True to form, Richie had been friends with the owner, John Lodano, from way back. About a week after talking to him, Richie was able to get her onto La Belle Maison's schedule in only four months. It cost her father a bit extra, actually, quite a bit extra, and it meant everything else needed to be speeded up, but it was worth it. She was able to work out a time for the ceremony with the church, and then she had to deal with her caterer, the great Chef Maurice, owner of Wholly Matrimony Caterers and renowned for his fabulous wedding feasts. For a generous bonus, she had gotten him not only to prepare Saturday's sit-down reception dinner, but Friday night's rehearsal dinner as well.

And that was where the problem came in.

She had arranged for the rehearsal dinner to be held on a small cruise ship that would sail around the bay while Chef Maurice served a delicious Italian meal. The wedding dinner wouldn't be Italian, but French, so she decided the rehearsal should be a nod to her family's ethnic heritage. She would also include Finnish desserts, a lingonberry pie and cloudberry mousse, in honor of Aulis Kokkonen, the man Paavo called his "step-father," who had raised Paavo after his mother had been forced to leave him. It wasn't until Paavo was an adult that he discovered the complete circumstances that caused him to end up with Aulis Kokkonen, and he appreciated the elderly Finnish man even more after learning the whole story and the dangers involved.

Chef Maurice had assured her the rehearsal dinner would be perfect. But now, she realized, the table setting was not.

She was tempted to call her sisters about the tragic lapse she had just discovered. Her four sisters had stepped in as her "wedding planners" when she couldn't find any professional planner who was able to meet her strict requirements. But now, they refused to discuss her wedding arrangements any longer. They told her in no uncertain terms that everything was going to run well.

"Well?" she had repeated. "*Well?* Since when is 'well' good enough?" Not in her book.

That was when they stopped answering her phone calls or text messages. She even posted messages to them on Facebook, but they also ignored those. She suspected they might even be laughing about her perfectionism. The nerve.

What should she do? The green sweater had reminded her that she had ordered little thank-you boxes of perfume for her bridesmaids and cologne for the groomsmen, and she planned to give them out during the Friday night rehearsal dinner. But the boxes would be wrapped in lime-green paper and tied with lime-green bows rather than the white paper and ribbon as she had originally thought. That meant she didn't want the caterer to use the lemon-yellow napkins she had chosen, but preferred that he use a white ones. She didn't want her table setting to look like an advertisement for citrus fruit.

Okay, even she had to admit that the color of giftwrap clashing with the color of table napkins was small, but she had wanted everything *to be perfect*. The thought of the imperfect table setting was like a toothache.

Since her sisters were ignoring her, she decided to take matters into her own hands and put in a call to Wholly Matrimony. No one answered, as expected that time of night.

She left a message. "This is Angie Amalfi. Something very important has come up regarding Friday night's dinner. Please call me as soon as possible." But then, before she hung up, she remembered her sisters saying not only would they no longer take any calls from her, they had told everyone else involved in putting on the wedding not to as well. What if Chef Maurice and his staff wouldn't answer her message? How vile was that?

"Or better yet"—the more she thought about her sisters telling the chef not to talk to her, the angrier she got—"I'll be there in the morning."

Chapter 4

Rebecca and Bill Sutter, who finally showed up at the crime scene, were seated in the events coordinator's office. It was a pretty room done in pastel blues and yellows giving it a French country flair. They sat at the small round table where Sally Lankowitz usually met with clients. Clearly, the office had been decorated to give potential customers a relaxed, welcome feeling.

Sutter nodded at Rebecca, indicating that although he was the senior homicide inspector, she was to take the lead on this case. He was in his late fifties, with short gray hair, watery gray eyes, and from the way he was acting since walking into the events hall, didn't like having anything to do with wedding receptions. He was divorced.

"Ms. Lankowitz," Rebecca said, her hands folded as she leaned slightly towards the woman, "I understand you were the one who stopped the guests from making a mad dash out the door. That was a good thing on your part. Now, could you please describe everything you saw and did?"

Sally shifted her red-framed glasses higher on her nose. She wore a plain but expensive black dress—the sort that would let her unobtrusively fit in with guests as she did her job. "I was looking for the bride because it was time for the cake cutting. I was surprised that she wasn't in the ballroom. I asked Leland, the groom, if he knew where she was, but he thought she was talking with one of the bridesmaids. I looked around, but I still didn't see her."

"Were all the bridesmaids in the ballroom?" Rebecca asked.

"I'm not sure. There were only three—it was a small wedding, as you saw. I'm not sure why they held it here, except that we're famous. But the bride paid for a lot more space than she needed, hiring this entire hall."

"And then what?"

"Well, I started walking around the room looking for her. Come to think of it, one of the bridesmaids may also have been missing. I know I saw two of them—their dresses are an ice blue shade—and I assumed the bride was with the third. I was heading for the stairs to check the ladies' room on the ground floor, when the door to the back of the hall swung open hard, and smacked loudly against the wall. The bride stumbled forward and kind of ran and staggered—my first thought was that she had overindulged—straight towards the cake." Sally took several deep breaths before continuing. "When she fell onto the cake, I saw the knife sticking out of her back. It was horrible! Beyond horrible. For a moment, I'm sorry to say, I froze."

"What happened after you saw her?"

"Well, as soon as the swinging doors banged against the walls, that caught everyone's attention. And when they saw the way Taylor was moving, several stood and watched. After she fell, it was pandemonium. The group surged towards her, with people shouting to call nine-one-one. But then someone screamed that she was dead. Several people turned as if to run from the place. Somehow, I thought to shout that they had to remain here, that we had to find out what had happened."

"Did they listen?"

Sally swallowed hard. "I'm not sure what would have happened if the best man hadn't spoken up. His name is Darrel Gruber. He said everyone needed to stay to put, that they needed to be there to support and help Leland Blythe, the groom. Leland, or Lee as his friends call him, had run to Taylor, and he was just standing next to her, not moving, not touching her, and looking completely shocked. At the best man's words, people quieted down and some agreed—or at least stayed put." A sudden tear began to roll down her cheek, and she brushed it away.

"That's good," Rebecca murmured, reminding herself that for a person like Sally Lankowitz who normally dealt with happy occasions, coming face-to-face with murder had to be traumatic. "So tell me, how did everyone end up downstairs?"

Sally tried hard to compose herself. "One of the attendees was a retired police officer. I think he was one of the groom's uncles or something. He told everyone they needed to go downstairs and wait for the police to arrive, and to clear the crime scene."

"So no one doubted she had been murdered?" Sutter asked, finally joining in the questioning.

"Not after seeing that knife in her back." Sally's answer was little more than a whisper, but then she faced Sutter with a question in her eyes. "Except that, how many brides are murdered on their wedding day? I tried to tell myself, and maybe others did as well, that she'd backed into the knife, or fell onto it somehow. But that's very hard to believe."

"True," Sutter said with a grimace.

Rebecca asked, "Did Taylor ever express anything to you that gave an indication she was worried or afraid of something happening at her wedding?"

"Quite the opposite." Sally pursed her lips. "She had been given a part in a movie, and everyone knew how excited she was to get the role."

"She was actress?" Rebecca asked.

"So she said. That was the reason for the Wednesday wedding. She needed to be on location in Mexico on Friday. The change was no problem for us. Wednesday is scarcely a busy day for weddings or any other receptions here."

"Was the date change a last minute thing?"

"We had a month's warning. We did our best, but Taylor was the type of bride who kept changing her mind and demanding that we jump through hoops to accommodate her every whim." Sally's jaw clenched, and she tightly clasped her hands together. "So much for all her demands now."

Rebecca and Bill Sutter took over the owner's office to hold interviews with the wedding party. It was far more formal, staid, and expensively decorated than Sally Lankowitz's. It was the sort of room, the two homicide inspectors decided, more likely to cause some nervousness in a guilty person.

Leland Blythe, the groom, was the first person they called in. He was about 5'9", medium build, with thinning brown hair with lots of gel to make the top stand in a skinny front-to-back fringe. He looked as if he was in a state of shock as he approached them. Both inspectors stood.

"I'm sorry for your loss," Rebecca and Sutter murmured. They introduced themselves and gestured towards a seat. He all but fell into it. They could smell the alcohol on his breath.

"Mr. Blythe," Rebecca began, "can you tell us where you were when you last saw Taylor?"

"Where? In the ballroom, of course."

"Did you talk to her?" Sutter asked.

"No. I was getting myself more champagne. Taylor doesn't like me to drink, but I really wanted to, so I went ahead. I didn't think she'd fuss at our wedding, after all. But I also didn't want to, like, shove it in her face."

"How long was that before ... before she stumbled into the room and onto the cake?" Rebecca tried to think of a better way to phrase that, but couldn't.

"I don't know. Fifteen, twenty minutes, I guess. I was talking to people."

"Who?"

"I don't know. A lot of them." He ran his fingers through his hair and then glared at the shiny goop that stuck to them. "I had my champagne, and I was being a good host, I guess.

"Did Taylor have any concerns about anyone wanting to harm her? Did she ever talk to you about anything like that?"

"Not at all." He began to choke up. "Everyone loved and admired her. The only problem could have been that some people were jealous of her. She was beautiful, successful, and was going to have a great career in movies."

"Do you think that's why your"—Sutter hesitated—"wife was murdered?"

Blythe's lips tightened. "All I know is someone murdered her. People don't stab themselves in the back, do they,

Inspector?"

"I haven't seen any members of her family here," Rebecca said. "Does she have any family?"

"She does." He didn't even attempt to hide the bitterness in his tone. "Her folks are in Chicago. Her mother was going to come, but at the last minute, her bitch sister Kaylee talked her mother into staying home. She said it wasn't worth the time or money it would take to travel to San Francisco since Taylor didn't have time to spend with her. Taylor was a very busy person, but she was furious that her sister would have interfered that way."

"So neither her mother or her sister, Kaylee, attended?" Rebecca asked.

"Correct."

"What do you think happened to Taylor?" Sutter abruptly asked. "Who wanted her dead?"

Blythe clenched his fists. "I don't know. I just don't know."

After Leland Blythe left, Rebecca and Sutter talked to his parents and his brother, Mason, who had come up to San Francisco from Los Angeles for the wedding. Each of them seemed completely baffled by everything that was going on. The only thing Rebecca picked up was that they didn't know Taylor very well. The brother only met her the day of the wedding, and the parents had only met her once before, even though they only lived thirty miles from the city. They had invited her to dinner many times, but she was always too busy to accept. Leland's mother seemed especially resentful of that, but it was hardly a killing matter.

The family was allowed to leave, and then Rebecca and Sutter quickly questioned the other guests, each taking half, saving the members of the wedding party for last.

It was getting close to two o'clock in the morning before they got to the bridesmaids and groomsmen. Between shock and booze, no one was thinking or speaking clearly. They had brought bottles of bourbon and scotch, plus a bag of ice, from the wet bar down to the living room, and proceeded to empty the liquor. They were soon sent home.

The kitchen staff was saved for last. The murder weapon had been a part of the knife set from the kitchen, and had been used to carve the roast beef that was served. No one could remember if it was returned to the kitchen after dinner with what remained of the roast beef, or if it had been left in the anteroom with other used cutlery.

Finally, the kitchen staff was also let go.

Alone in the office, Rebecca and Sutter faced each other. They were also tired, and sat on each end of the leather sofa that graced the room. "What do you think?" Sutter asked, rubbing his eyes.

"Other than the groom, I didn't see one honest tear over Taylor's death." Rebecca put her elbow on the sofa's arm and rested her head in her hand.

"I noticed. Very strange, considering they're supposed to be her close friends."

"But they weren't. They were people she would be working with on a movie."

"Yeah, some movie." Sutter smirked. "*Outbreak.* It sounds like a movie about acne, not people from outer space who eat steel, and as a result, destroy our skyscrapers, bridges, and appliances. Why doesn't anybody make good movies anymore like *Doctor Zhivago?*"

Rebecca did a double-take. Did Sutter actually have a heart?

"Those bridesmaids were odd," Rebecca said, sitting straight again and trying to clear her head. "Not close to her at all."

"No one was," Sutter said. "Except the groom."

One of the questions they always asked each individual when dealing with a group, was who they were with at the moment of the "incident."

"Did you find anyone who was alone or talking to no one?" Rebecca asked.

"Nope," Sutter said. "Everyone said he or she was talking with someone else. As far as I can tell, although I'll go over my notes again later, all the so-called clusters of conversations seemed to back each other up. But both the groom's buddies and the movie people were really packing away the booze, and probably started doing so long before the murder. So they could have been talking to the wall, for all some of them knew."

"Agreed. But if they're right in what they told you, we've got a murder that took place in a room where the bride was supposedly alone—although why she would go into that room was anybody's guess—she was stabbed, no one cared but the groom, and all of them had alibis. Does that sum it up so far?"

Sutter nodded. "It does."

Rebecca frowned. "That's what I was afraid of."

The two walked down the hall to see John Lodano, the owner. He was the only person not connected with police work who remained. A heavy-set, balding man, with a large head and hang-dog expression, he sat in the reception area, seated on a sofa and drinking coffee to stay awake. He had left the wedding after the dinner was served to go home and nap while cake, toasts, and dancing were going on. He had planned to return after the party ended to oversee the clean-up, but Sally Lankowitz's startling phone call had changed those plans.

"You can go home, now, Mr. Lodano," Rebecca said. "We'll contact you if we need any more information. The Crime Scene Unit will be here for a few more hours tonight. You've met the lead detective, Inspector Hwang. He'll make sure everything is locked up when they leave. This building is now a sealed crime scene, and everyone will need to stay out of it. We'll let you know as soon as we can release it back to you."

"You've got to be kidding." Lodano's body seemed to swell up as he spoke. "What do you mean stay out? How long? I have wedding receptions coming up. Big ones, on both Saturday and Sunday."

"We'll release it as soon as possible, but it all depends on how the investigation goes. If we quickly find the killer, we'll open it immediately. If not, we may need to hold onto it until we know we've checked everything. This is such a large facility, with so many nooks and crannies, that it might take a while."

"How long," Lodano asked, his voice low and deadly, "is a while?"

"We understand the importance of reopening your business." Rebecca tried to calm him. "I promise we'll be as prompt as possible, but we must be thorough. Usually we keep the crime scene no more than three or four days. We'll try to have it back to you by Monday or Tuesday."

"How can I disappoint my customers who have been planning their wedding receptions here for months and months?" he bellowed. "I need to have my hall back."

"I'm sorry, but a woman was murdered here tonight." Rebecca's words were firm, her gaze every bit as lethal as his had been to her. "Catching her killer takes precedence over a party. Or don't you agree?"

He shut his mouth and walked ahead of her out the door.

Chapter 5

Angie awoke earlier that morning filled with cheer, enthusiasm, and love of the world, despite having to go to Wholly Matrimony with new napkins to take care of the lemon/lime color situation.

But, she had reasoned as she got ready to go out, this trip would give her a chance to double-check that everything was in place for the big sit-down wedding reception dinner. Since she was, after all, a gourmet cook who had studied at the Cordon Bleu in Paris, everyone expected a delicious meal, and that was what she intended to give them.

She had requested that each table have a collection of French cheeses, a classic goose liver pâté, and French bread. She planned the meal to begin with escargot, followed by French onion soup, then scallops (Coquilles St. Jacques), a mixed-green salad with buttermilk and crème fraiche dressing, and after that, a main course of veal in cream sauce with wild rice. For dessert, the guests would be served apricot clafoutis topped with whipped cream and sliced almonds. After dinner, there would be dancing, which should work up an appetite for a slice of the gargantuan wedding cake she had ordered made with rum-flavored Italian cream.

She was just about to leave the apartment when the phone rang. She happened to glance at the clock as she took her cell phone out of her handbag—9:28 a.m. A time that would live in infamy.

"Caller ID" told her the call was from John Lodano, the owner of La Belle Maison. Alarm bells went off as she saw his name, but she told herself he was only calling to tell her how thrilled he was to host her wedding reception on Saturday. A charming and gracious gesture, nothing more.

The bells, however, turned into a full scale siren when he asked if he could stop by her apartment that very morning for a "discussion."

"What discussion?" she had demanded.

"It'll take me ten minutes and I'll be right over," Lodano said, which did nothing to lessen her nerves.

The man who arrived at her apartment was quite different from the suave self-important fellow she met briefly at La Belle Maison before she'd been turned over to Sally Lankowski. He looked beyond nervous as she invited him into the living room and had him sit.

She guessed he had broken the news as gently as possible, all things considered. But how gently could one explain to a bride that her long-awaited wedding reception location had been declared a crime scene? Especially when he was forced to include that, unless the police released it, she was going to have to find another location for her reception.

She had stared at him in speechless, open-mouthed

wonder. *Oh, certainly, Mr. Lodano. It's no problem at all to find a location for three hundred people in less than two days.*

Finally, she managed to croak out, "What do you mean, a crime scene? What happened?"

Lodano went pale. His hands shook and he was visibly sweating. "There was a-a-a death. I'm sorry to say."

"A death?" she repeated. "What, someone choked on the food? Slipped and fell? What?"

"No, it was a little more serious. It"—he stuck two fingers in the knot at his tie and waggled it loose—"it might have been murder."

"Murder?" The word came out so shrill and sharp it could have etched glass.

He nodded.

She thought a moment. "Okay, that might not be so bad."

Lodano gawked. "Not bad?"

"I mean, not that it's good. What I'm trying to say is my husband-to-be is a homicide inspector. He might even have the case. I'm sure he'll move heaven and earth to get me the reception hall of my dreams. I'll talk to him."

Lodano looked skeptical. "It might not happen. I mean, the detectives there last night sounded very—"

"Who was there?"

He pulled out two SFPD business cards and read the names. "Rebecca Mayfield and Bill Sutter."

Angie stiffened. She knew Bill Sutter wouldn't be a problem. The man would fold like a cheap lawn chair and release the crime scene as soon as any pressure to do so was put on him. Rebecca Mayfield, however, was another story. She was notoriously by-the-book, and besides, she didn't exactly approve of Paavo marrying Angie.

Angie folded her arms. Over the years, she had been quite sure Inspector Mayfield wanted Paavo for herself. Short, brunette Angie had spent a lifetime feeling second fiddle to tall, buxom blondes from the time Jimmy Soares asked Dinah Turner to the Junior Prom instead of her. It had broken her heart. But it must have been true love because, years later, the two got married. Still, Angie couldn't help but laugh out loud when she realized that from that day forward the bane of young Angie's life would be known as Dinah Soares.

This time, however, Angie had gotten her man, despite the attractive blond he worked with.

She all but drilled a hole into Lodano's head with her eyes. "Somehow, my wedding reception will take place in your facility."

She watched his Adam's apple bob several times. He pulled out a handkerchief to wipe his sopping brow. "I suggest ... just to be safe, mind you ... that you contact your caterer and warn him there might be a change in plans."

Angie shut her eyes. She hated to admit it, but he might be right. From all she'd heard about Rebecca.... *Damn! Why did it have to be Mayfield on the case?*

"I guess so," she said. "But I don't see how I'm going to find another place in this short amount of time."

Lodano jumped to his feet. "You might try outside the city. I'm truly sorry. And please tell your Cousin Richie that it wasn't my fault, okay? It wasn't my fault."

Angie walked him to the door. "Okay, it's not your fault. But how maddening! Tell me, who was it who was killed?"

Lodano hesitated, then said softly, "I'm sure the name will mean nothing to you."

"Still ..."

He ran a thick tongue over his lower lip. "A young woman, Taylor Redmun."

Angie gasped, and without thinking blurted, "Somebody killed Bridezilla?"

Lodano nodded. "I'm afraid so." Then, realizing what he had just admitted to, he began stuttering and stammering to make up for his mistake.

They quickly said good-bye, and as Angie shut the door, she couldn't help but think she could name a prime suspect: Sally Lankowitz.

Again alone, Angie sat on the petit-point sofa in the living room. Her feet were flat on the floor, her hands in her lap, as she stared at the wall across the room and tried to process all that John Lodano had told her. She was in shock. Complete, unadulterated shock.

She hadn't liked Bridezilla, but the thought of a bride, any bride, being killed on her wedding day was horrible. She felt bad about that. Adding that Bridezilla had been killed at La Belle Maison felt kind of creepy, all things considered.

But right now, Angie had her own wedding plans to think

about. The reception guest list stood at nearly three-hundred people.

And after the visit she had just received, her blood pressure was probably double that.

Her world had been turned upside-down. As she sat too stunned to move, across her mind danced all the little things that had bothered her—like napkin colors—and she realized how foolishly inconsequential they were.

She had two choices: to sit here feeling sorry for herself, or to do something about it.

Angie was never one to sit still.

She rushed straight to the Hall of Justice, a broad gray cement building located amidst ugly freeway exits and entrances just south of downtown San Francisco. The Hall held courtrooms, cells belonging to the city's jail system, and the police department's Bureau of Inspections.

She went straight to the Homicide Division on the fourth floor. This was too important for phone or text messages. This required face-to-face communication. And maybe tears.

Angie knew Homicide's secretary, and waved to Elizabeth as she hurried past her into the bureau's main room. It was big and messy with desks piled high with papers, binders, files, and computer monitors. On the edges were the interrogation rooms and the chief's office.

Paavo was at his desk when she stormed in. His partner and best man, Toshiro Yoshiwara, aka Yosh, was also there, as was Luis Calderon. The other three inspectors, Mayfield, Sutter, and Calderon's partner, Bo Benson, were out—hopefully trying to determine who killed Bridezilla so she could get her wedding reception venue back.

Paavo stood as she entered, looking surprised, but handsome as always. Tall, broad shouldered, with a slim build, he had short, dark brown hair, high cheekbones, a firm mouth, and the palest large blue eyes she had ever seen. It was those eyes that first caught her attention, well, no—it was the body, then the handsome face—but the eyes were the icing on the cake.

She couldn't think about his looks now. She had a disaster to avert.

"Angie! What a surprise. Is something wrong?"

"You haven't heard, I take it." At his quizzical look, she sat down on the guest chair beside his desk. "Where is Rebecca Mayfield?"

He sat as well, scooting his chair closer to hers. "I suspect she's out working the case she and Bill Sutter got hit with last night. They're the on-call team this week."

Angie nodded. "So, they haven't solved it yet?"

"I guess not, but why are you asking?"

"What are they doing now?"

"What's going on, Angie?"

"Please, Paavo."

He grew more confused with each non-answer she gave. Finally, he stopped asking questions. His face stern, he said, "I haven't heard anything. They were apparently up most of the night, and haven't come in yet this morning. Tell me why you want to know. Is someone you know involved?"

Angie drew in her breath and shut her eyes a moment, wondering how to break the terrible news to him. She took his hand in both of hers, but the words wouldn't come.

"Angie," he said softly, worried, "what's wrong? I want to know what's happened."

She drew in her breath again, and then held his gaze. "I had met the victim. She was ... she was Bridezilla."

"What?" He looked pained.

Like a drain unplugged, the words gushed from her. "Bridezilla. You know, the obnoxious bride I told you about. The one who interrupted so much when I was talking to Sally Lankowitz, our wedding consultant at La Belle Maison, I had to reschedule. And ... and ..." Angie's eyes filled with tears as the enormity of what happened hit her. How could she ever tell Paavo what a disaster their wedding day had become?

He put his free hand on her narrow shoulder and gave an affectionate squeeze. "Angie, don't let it upset you. I'm sorry the person you met was killed, but it has nothing to do with you as a bride. If there's some weird superstition about it, it's just a superstition. Things will be all right."

His words made no sense. How silly did he think she was? The more she thought about it, the more annoyed she became. She let go of his hand, her cheeks flaming. "A superstition? Is that what you think is troubling me? What? Something old, new, dead and blue? Is that it? Or maybe it's the one that says don't hang around dead brides before your wedding."

"Angie, take a deep breath." She knew he wanted to sound soothing, but she grew more irritated with each word. "I can imagine that meeting a bride and now learning that she's dead is a trifle, well, more than a trifle upsetting and—"

"Paavo, stop! Our wedding reception venue is the crime scene."

He gawked at her. "No."

"Yes. La Belle Maison. The place I worked like a dog to get for our reception; the place I finally had to ask Cousin Richie for help in finding a space for us on their calendar. It's now the crime scene, and if the murder isn't solved by Saturday at 4 p.m., no, actually they'll need time to set things up—if it isn't solved by Saturday at noon, we won't have a place for our reception. We have three hundred people coming to see us get married, and we have no place to feed them."

As the full impact of what she was saying hit, as he thought of the untold hours she had spent obsessing over her Big Day, Paavo shook his head. "I'm so sorry, Angie."

"Sorry?" she cried. "Paavo, you've got to fix this."

He gaped. "I don't know if I can."

"You've got to. Find the killer. Open up the crime scene. Or even if you don't find the killer, you can surely get CSI to finish what they're doing before Saturday. I mean, how long can it take to spread around a little fingerprint dust?"

He rubbed his temples. "I don't know."

"Does Mayfield know it's the place for our wedding reception?"

"I don't know, Angie."

Angie folded her arms. "Surely, she wouldn't want to mess up your wedding day, would she?"

"Angie, you know Rebecca isn't like that."

"Do I?"

"Ask Cousin Richie. He seems to like her well enough," Paavo said.

"Richie likes women. Enough said. Anyway, what if we, I mean, if Rebecca finds out who killed Bridezilla before Saturday, will that free up La Belle Maison so we could still have our reception there?"

"If she gets a confession, and no trial, perhaps. But the chance of all that happening in forty-eight hours is close to impossible. I suggest you start looking elsewhere. Speaking of Cousin Richie, he's got a nightclub."

"Yes, a nightclub, not a wedding reception venue. And I had my heart set on La Belle Maison! I don't want to even consider moving until all else fails."

"Do we *need* a reception?" he asked.

She looked at him with horror, and then tears filled her eyes. "I had wanted this to be perfect. Everything to be perfect—for you, as well as me." She brushed away foolish tears. "I'll call my sisters. We'll start making phone calls right away. Maybe we'll be lucky and some couple will have had a big fight and canceled their wedding. Or, we can at least hope."

Paavo stood and helped her to her feet. "All right," he said. "I'll track down Rebecca and Bill and find out what's going on. I'm sure we'll be able to work out something. Go home, and don't worry."

He walked her to the elevator, where he kissed her and held her and told her their wedding reception would be fine.

The elevator doors opened, and she got on.

"Thank you," she said with a bright smile. "That's all I needed to hear."

"Oh, but just in case"—he called as the doors drew shut— "you'd better make a back-up plan."

Chapter 6

As soon as Angie left, Paavo phoned Rebecca and learned she was at the victim's apartment looking for anything that would give her some clue as to who would want to kill Taylor Redmun-Blythe, aka Bridezilla. He told her he'd like to come over.

"Why am I not surprised," she said, and hung up.

The apartment was located near the waterfront, just off Broadway Street, which sounded a lot better than it actually was. Wharf rats, the four-legged kind, were common in the area. The apartment itself was tiny with worn furniture, not the sort of place he expected for someone whose wedding had been held at the very expensive La Belle Maison. He guessed the groom was the one with money.

Rebecca folded her arms as Paavo walked into the apartment. "So, Angie called in the cavalry, I take it. Richie called to warn me that her wedding reception is at risk, and I seem to be the road block."

He was stunned. "Richie knew before I did?"

"He said something about the owner talking to him. It's not important."

"Look, I'm sorry," he said. "But you know Angie. She had her heart set ..." He stopped talking. As Rebecca's frown and irritation seemed too grow, just as had happened earlier when he tried to calm Angie, he realized every word he said was having the opposite effect from what he had hoped. Why, he wondered, was it always so much easier to talk to his partner, Yosh? "I'm only here to see if there's anything I can help with, anything I can do to speed this up—"

"No." She went back into the bedroom to continue going through the victim's closet.

Paavo followed. "Where's Sutter?"

"He's talking one more time to the groom's parents," Rebecca said.

"Have you learned anything about the victim that gives some idea of why she was killed?"

Rebecca shut the closet door. She had found nothing in there. She walked over to a nightstand, but before opening the drawer faced Paavo. "Not yet. But it was actually a strange wedding. Each of her bridesmaids was surprised to have been asked to take part. None were close friends with her. In fact, I couldn't find anyone who was—other than the groom. Her own family hadn't bothered to attend."

He thought of Angie's relatives flying and driving in from all over the country. And many of them were people he'd never even heard her mention. "That's surprising."

"Her sister lives in Berkeley. Sutter and I went to visit her early this morning to break the news to her. She was sad more for her parents' sake than anything. Her parents live in

Chicago, Taylor's hometown, but they haven't seen each other in years."

"Did the sister say why?"

"Nothing specific. To paraphrase, 'Taylor was a selfish bitch, and always has been'."

Paavo nodded. He'd heard similar tales about families plenty of times. Considering his own miserable experience with family, and what he'd seen on the job, how well Angie's family got along with each other actually surprised him. "Any ideas as to who might have killed her?"

"No, nothing other than it was almost certainly someone in attendance at the wedding. At least, no one saw any strangers enter or leave the building, and it was a small group so someone not belonging would most likely have been noticed. But I've requested the venue's security cameras as well as any other in the immediate area to double check that. In any case, at the moment, we have two theories. Either Taylor went to meet someone in the anteroom—a sort of a pantry that leads to the service elevator downstairs to the kitchen—and that person killed her; or she decided to use the elevator instead of the stairs to go down to the women's room, and someone waited in the anteroom for her to return and killed her. My gut tells me the last is less likely. Too much left to chance."

"Who would she be meeting in secret at her wedding?" Paavo asked.

"I have no idea. Yet."

He nodded. "Looking at the wedding party and the guests, does anyone stand out?"

"The main thing standing out is that everyone was family or a friend of the groom, or a *business* associate of the bride. The business associates—her agent and people involved in a movie Taylor was going to be in—seemed to hardly know her. After a murder, people usually talk about what a saint the deceased was. In this case, they talked about how they wished they hadn't come to the wedding, except that it was on a Wednesday night and they didn't really have an excuse not to. Apparently, in 'show biz,' as one of them said, you never know when someone's career will take off, so it's best not to burn bridges."

"Sounds like a caring bunch," Paavo said.

"Very. But it also sounds like a bunch of people with no reason to kill her."

"Unless someone saw her as potential competition."

"Could be."

"What are you doing next, Rebecca?"

"I asked the members of the wedding to be at the bureau at one. Sutter and I will interview them individually. That might help us get to the bottom of this mess."

"And the crime scene unit?"

She shook her head. "The knife was from the kitchen, brought to the ballroom to carve the roast beef, and somehow ended up in the bride's back. Her fingerprints are all over the facility, including the kitchen, and they're trying to determine who else's were with her."

"Has anyone looked into the caterer?" Paavo asked.

"Not yet."

"If you can use the help ..."

Before she answered, her phone buzzed. It was Homicide's dispatcher. After talking a moment, she shook her head. "Great. Another dead body. This one was found under very mysterious circumstances—and she's wearing a wedding dress."

"What?" Paavo could hardly believe it.

"Sutter and I are the on-call team this week. We'll have to go over there." San Francisco Homicide used a system where two-person "on-call" teams handled all homicides in a given week or weekend, and then concentrated on working those homicide cases until their next on-call turn came up. Only rarely did so many unrelated homicides occur in any given period that the on-call team couldn't handle them.

Paavo knew that if Rebecca and Sutter went to look into this new case, the Redmun-Blythe murder investigation would take a temporary back seat. Even if they found that this latest call didn't involve a murder, it could chew up enough time to make it almost impossible to solve the Redmun-Blythe murder before Saturday.

"If you'd like," he said, "Yosh and I will handle the call for you. But if there's any way the death is connected with this bride—"

"You mean like some deranged wedding-hating serial killer running through our city?'

"Exactly, God-help us. If that's the situation, we'll work the cases together."

"You know I really should tell you to take a flying leap and keep your nose out of my cases," she said, hands on hips.

"But you understand that this is a rare circumstance, and I'm a truly desperate man."

She nodded, and seemed unable to stop a smile from playing across her lips. "Yes. And, I've come to understand the Amalfis a bit. Not, let me say, that I particularly like them, but I can sympathize with what you're facing."

All he could say was, "Thank you, Rebecca."

Paavo contacted Yosh and met his partner ten minutes later in the area known as the Western Addition. It was near downtown, and some of it had been gentrified over the past few years, while other parts had fallen into decay and neglect.

Toshiro Yoshiwara had become Paavo's partner some time earlier after transferring to San Francisco from Seattle—and after Paavo's former partner had been murdered. Yosh, as everyone called him, was large for a Japanese, tall, with broad shoulders, a massive chest, and a head that seemed a little small for all that body. He wore his hair in a short buzz cut, and looked like he could split a house in two and not raise a sweat. He was also the extrovert to Paavo's introvert. He shook hands, shot the bull, and easily conversed with people, winning their confidence and getting them at ease enough to talk. He could work a room in a way Paavo had never seen before, and—to use one of Yosh's favorite phrases—people ate it up like a Hershey bar.

Now, a group of mostly African-Americans stood on the sidewalk watching the police. They stepped aside to open a corridor for Paavo and Yosh to enter the large, public housing apartment building. Yosh, as usual, greeted everyone as he walked by, while Paavo kept his expression stern. The uniformed policeman guarding the crime scene introduced them to Benny Simms, the building manager, who had called the police earlier that day. Simms was white, probably in his forties, a forlorn forties, with a chalky complexion, and none-too-clean dark blond hair.

He led Paavo and Yosh through the basement to the store room where the body had been found.

As soon as Paavo saw the corpse, he realized that if the same person had killed Taylor Redmun-Blythe, the perpetrator's rage against brides had lasted a long time, and his MO had completely changed.

"My God." Yosh gazed with disgust and more than a little horror at the sight of the desiccated female. She lay on her back on a filthy bed wearing a bridal gown with a white bridal veil covering some of her black hair, but not her face.

The worst part was the thick pink lipstick on her mouth—lipstick that looked moist and eerily fresh.

"How did you find her?" Paavo asked.

Simms twitched as he spoke. "I never come down here 'less a furnace conks out or some such. Most all these rooms is kept locked up."

"What is this room?" Yosh asked.

"It's s'posed to be empty—a store room, but people here don't have nothing much to store, so it ain't used."

"Why did you look inside?" Paavo asked.

"One of the tenants told me somebody was hanging around down here. I figured I'd better check it out. Junkies and homeless try to break in all the time. Make it a crib, you know? Get out of the cold, away from the cops. Kids, too. Or gangs. I don't know. Anyway, when I was checking things out, I found her."

"Any idea who she is?"

"Hell, no."

"Who else had access to this room?"

"Anybody who lives here could come down," Simms said. "Or their friends. Or whoever wants to break in. It ain't hard." A thin sheen of nervous perspiration glistened on his upper lip and brow. "It ain't my fault if somebody gets in. I mean, managers might have had a duplicate key made and kept it. I got two, but I never give none to nobody."

"Did you ever see anyone down here? Any of your tenants, or other people?" Paavo asked.

Simms used his fingers to wipe the sweat trickling along his temple, then wiped them on his jeans. "No. I don't think so. Not that I remember, anyways. Nobody has no reason to come down here 'less it's for no good."

Paavo nodded at Yosh to take over the questioning as he perused the storeroom.

"Was the door to the storeroom locked?" Yosh asked.

"No. I locked it last time I was here. But this time, somebody left it unlocked," Simms replied, eyeballing Paavo who was walking around the room.

"When were you last in here?" Yosh asked.

"Shit, I don't know. Maybe six, seven months ago. Like I said, it's supposed to be empty. No reason for me to come in here."

"Which tenant told you he heard someone down here?"

"Hell, man, I don't know. I got a note. People here don't talk much, especially not to rat out each other. It's a rough neighborhood."

Yosh was growing increasingly irritated. "How long have you been manager?"

"Uh ... about nine months, I guess."

"How did you get the job?"

"I heard, if I did it, I didn't have to pay no rent. I went down to City Hall. Nobody else wanted it."

Paavo wasn't surprised at that answer. He could understand no one wanting to be responsible for trying to keep tenants in a building like this happy. It would be a thankless task. He faced Simms, and gestured towards the high, transom window. "Why is that window black?" he asked.

The landlord looked at it and gaped. "Oh, shit. I didn't even notice."

"Are all the windows down here painted?"

"Maybe. I never paid no attention."

They heard footsteps and talking outside the door, and soon Evelyn Ramirez, the M.E., stepped into the room. As usual with Evelyn, when she entered a crime scene with her bustling entourage of assistants, the attention turned her way. She walked up to the corpse. "What's this? Someone have a grudge against marriage?" She bent close. "If so, the grudge has gone on for a long time."

"Any chance to get fingerprints?" Paavo asked.

She looked at the hand. "I'll try to rehydrate the skin. So, yes, there's a chance. Just not a big one." She shook her head. "Poor Paavo. What a pair of murders to face the week before your wedding day!"

"I know," Paavo said glumly. "And the one last night was at the place Angie chose for our reception. I don't know what we're going to do. It's a big hall and it's all now a crime scene. Angie's having fits."

"You've got time," Evelyn said. "Things have a way of working out for the best sometimes."

"I hope so," Paavo muttered.

He and Yosh stepped outside the storeroom, leaving it for the M.E. and the Crime Scene Investigators. They knew they had a lot of work to do, canvassing the tenants in the apartment and the neighborhood to see if anyone saw anything that might give some clue as to who the woman was, and who had visited her recently enough to apply some lipstick that hadn't yet dried out.

Chapter 7

Angie went to the Wings of an Angel restaurant on Columbus Avenue in the North Beach area. It was owned by three older men, ex-cons, who had become good and true friends to her. She sat over a plate of their signature spaghetti, one with a surprisingly delicious sauce. Angie had been shocked to learn the secret, completely non-Italian ingredient they used in it: Spam®. But this afternoon, the noodles might have been string for all the attention she gave them.

"Whatza matter, Miss Angie?" Earl White, one of the owners, sat down across from her as soon as the last of the lunch crowd left the restaurant. Earl was in his sixties, and wore a thick, curly-brown toupee so stiff it looked as if it had been shellacked. He'd once worked as a bouncer in Las Vegas. But the job didn't last too long, since, tough as he was, five-foot-five bouncers sometimes got bounced themselves.

"A murder was committed at the place I plan to hold my wedding reception," Angie explained. "Now, the whole building is a crime scene. For me to use it, Homicide will need to release the scene by noon on Saturday. I don't know if they'll be able to do it."

Earl's eyebrows rose. "Geez, t'at's a bad break. I'm sure sorry to hear it. But you'll find anot'er place, I'm sure. An' you still got your caterer, right? That Maurice guy? I shoulda known you'd get somebody big an' popular like him to cook for your weddin'. My mouth waters jus' t'inkin' about it. An' t'ank you for the invite. Me, Butch, and Vinnie ain't never been to a fancy shindig like you're puttin' on. We appreciate you t'inkin' of us."

"Of course, I'd invite you guys. I love you!"

"We love you, too, Miss Angie." He then blushed.

"Thank you. But the problem is, I've phoned a bunch of places, and every other venue that could hold three-hundred people at a sit-down dinner is booked up. I have no idea what to do."

"I wish our place was bigger. You coulda used it for free. But only about"—he looked over the six tables—"t'irty or so people could fit here. But if t'ere's anyt'ing we can do ..."

She glanced over the empty dining area, a small, cozy room with wood-stained walls and big, round, white light fixtures. When Wings of an Angel first opened, she'd helped make it inviting by putting up pretty lace curtains and having the owners replace gray Formica tables and aluminum chairs with wooden ones. She also remembered the first time she came in here. She'd being drawn to the restaurant because of its lovely, ethereal name. Then she learned the ex-cons named it after an old song that was dear to them—one in which the singer said if he had the wings of an angel, he'd fly over the prison walls surrounding him.

So much for her romantic thoughts about its name.

"I know you'd like to help, Earl. Thank you."

As Earl stood to leave Angie to her food, Richie Amalfi sauntered into the restaurant.

Angie's father and Richie's were brothers, but Richie's life had been very different from Angie's privileged one. His father was killed when he was quite young, and he was an only child, raised by his mother, Carmela, who had never remarried. Then, four years earlier, his fiancée died in an auto accident. That sent him on a downhill spiral, drinking too much, eating all the wrong foods, and generally not taking care of himself at all until friends and family somehow managed to pull him out of it.

He was now nearing forty and was, to Angie's eye, quite handsome with black hair, soulful brown eyes, and standing fit and trim after straightening out his diet and exercising. On top of that, he was always impeccably dressed, sharing Angie's appreciation for good clothes and Italian shoes. She could tell from the cut that his gray sports coat was an Armani. With it, he wore a light blue shirt, no tie, black slacks, and buttery-soft black leather loafers.

He treated Angie as if she were the little sister he never had, and she loved him without reservation. But to many others, he seemed a bit shady—probably because no one knew exactly how he made his money.

He was often Angie's go-to guy when she needed something "fixed"—and she didn't mean mechanically. Richie always seemed to "know a guy who knows a guy" to take care of problems. Normally, she would have called him for help, the way she did about getting on La Maison Belle's calendar. But Angie feared that, this time, not even Cousin Richie's magic could help her out. Still, she couldn't help but smile and even feel a little relief to see him coming towards her.

"'Ey Richie," Earl said as the two shook hands.

"Good to see you, Earl. How about a glass of chianti and a menu while I see what's up with my glum cousin?"

"Good luck," Earl muttered as he scurried away.

Richie and Angie exchanged quick kisses on the cheek, then he sat at her table. "I just heard. I'm so sorry, Angie." He eyed her food. "That looks good."

"Here." She slid her plate towards him. "I can't eat."

Earl brought him silverware and sour-dough bread along with his wine, and kept the menu.

"Thanks, Earl," Richie said, then faced Angie again. "So, tell me what's going on."

As he ate, Angie gave him a quick run-down of her past few days, beginning with meeting Bridezilla.

"So now," Richie said, twirling spaghetti onto his fork, "if Homicide can figure out who the murderer is, your wedding is back on track?"

She nodded. "I understand all that's needed is for them to declare the venue no longer a crime scene, and it's mine."

"But if they can't ..." He shook his head. "My club is big enough, but it's booked for late afternoon and early evening by a big fund-raiser for new equipment for the cancer wing at Children's Hospital. It's not like I can toss them."

"No—and I wouldn't want you to. What I want, what I've

always wanted, is La Belle Maison. Oh—John Lodano wants to make sure you know it's not his fault that I might not get it. What's that all about, Richie?"

"Nothing! He's a friend, that's all."

She couldn't help but wonder.

He asked, "I understand Rebec—, uh, Inspector Mayfield, is in charge of the case?"

Angie's eyes narrowed. Something about the way he said Rebecca's name was different. "That's right." She cocked an eyebrow. "Did you know that your mother told my mother that you and Rebecca Mayfield were getting a bit chummy?"

He smiled, then gave a "who cares?" shrug. His smile, however, never reached his eyes. It vanished completely as he said, "Yeah, well, that was a while ago. We're completely opposite in everything. I mean, everything. She's a cop, for one thing."

Angie wasn't buying it. "You can charm the pants off anyone, and you know it."

He looked stunned. "Uh, not the Inspector."

Angie reddened. "Oh, I didn't mean it that way! It was just a figure of speech."

Richie leaned back in his chair and chuckled. "It's okay, little cousin. Don't worry about Mayfield and me. We're just friends. But friends is good. I'll see what I can find out. Do you know the bride's name?"

"Yes. Taylor Redmun."

From the open kitchen door came owner Vinnie Freiman's voice. "Taylor?"

Angie and Richie glanced at each other, realizing Vinnie—and probably Earl and Butch, the third owner—had been listening to their conversation.

"That's what she said," Richie called. "Why?"

Vinnie shuffled towards them. He was no taller than Earl, and equally stocky. He wore no toupee, but was bald. The bags under his eyes had bags, making him look perpetually exhausted. "I wasn't listenin'. Swear. I was passin' by when I heard the name."

"And?" Richie asked.

Vinnie gulped. "She useta come here all the time. She baked the chocolate torte we useta sell for dessert. But mosta the money she made sellin' them to us went to food and wine. After a while, she stopped bakin' tortes, but still came by to eat and drink. She was always sayin' the cakes would be comin' soon. But they never did, and when she owed us over two-Cs in chocolate cake, we cut her off."

"What do you know about her?"

"Not much. The dame could turn on the charm when she wanted to, but mostly she was a cold fish. Yolanda at the Blue Velvet Pub down on Columbus could tell you better'n me. She's a cocktail waitress, and she and Taylor were tight. Taylor worked there, too, for a while. Heard she got booted for snortin' too much nose candy. Maybe true, maybe not. Anyhow, we thought she'd pay us for the dinners we gave her. But she never did, the mooch."

"Thanks, Vinnie." Richie said, then faced Angie. "How'd you like a Brandy Alexander?"

She raised her eyebrows, then smiled. "I know just the place to get one."

With that, the two cousins left.

Benny Simms stood on the street in front of the apartment building he was supposed to manage. If he'd known what it was like to live there, he'd have demanded that the city not only give him rent, but pay him besides. As it was now, he pretended to manage the place, and the city pretended to value him for his job.

He watched as the police van drove away with the bride. His bride. Then he hurried into the building to his studio apartment.

In it, he had three prized possessions: a TV, a computer, and a printer—a laser so he didn't have to keep ripping off Staples to buy ink cartridges. Those toners lasted forever.

Other than that, the apartment was filled with papers, magazines, used wrappings from fast-food joints, and he wasn't even sure what else. Probably the rats knew better than he did. He had to fight them for space on his sofa and bed. Every so often, he'd get sick of the mess and throw everything into a black garbage bag, but right now, he was glad that feeling hadn't come over him for at least two or three months. Maybe longer.

Eventually he found the papers he was looking for—a stack of wedding announcements printed off the *San Francisco Chronicle's* "Union Squared" online site—a name most likely only appreciated, with a pun only understood, by residents in or around the city. It was cute.

Cute things were stupid.

Weddings were stupid. And brides were the dumbest of all.

Ever since he'd heard that the homicide detective in charge of figuring out who or what had killed Shawnita was getting married this weekend, he'd been pissed. The damned cop took away Shawnita, and now he expected to go running off with his own bride to spend a happy honeymoon. Where was the justice in that?

Simms had come to love Shawnita over the months they'd been together in their special place in the basement. He could talk to her, and although he knew she was dead—he wasn't crazy—he could also feel her spirit near him, understanding him like no one ever had. He knew she had come to love him the way he did her.

And now, that piece of crap detective was sending her to a morgue where she'd be sliced up like a dead animal.

He looked at the card the man had given him: Paavo Smith. Then he turned to the wedding announcements.

Wedding announcements had interested him long before he met Shawnita. Plastic smiles on faces looking into the camera. Most of them somehow managed to show expressions filled with hope for a bright future—a future that everyone knew was a farce. And bright? Hah. He liked to look at the announcements and laugh at all the stupid people in them.

Stupid people made him sick. The world would be better off without them.

Shawnita had been lucky. She'd never made it to the altar, so she didn't have to go through with the whole wedding charade, a charade that ended in more misery than anyone should have to bear. Joy was fleeting, only sorrow stayed, crushing a person under its weight.

He had never married. He was too smart for that.

One by one, he went through the announcements until he found the one he sought: Amalfi-Smith.

He studied the photo and the write-up, especially the image of the bride. Angelina Amalfi. Then, he smiled.

She would have been a gorgeous bride, he thought. He looked for the date of the marriage to confirm it was this coming Saturday. It was, which meant he had time. Not a lot, but enough. First, he needed to find out where she lived.

He thought about the storage room that was now empty. Soon, it would be filled once again with love. Come to think of it, this new bride was a lot prettier than the old one.

The cop should thank him for what he was about to do, and would. In time.

Chapter 8

Angie felt really good after she and Cousin Richie found Taylor's former friend and had a long talk with her. She went straight to Homicide to tell Paavo everything she'd learned about Taylor Redmun, but he wasn't there. Instead, Inspector Calderon told her Paavo was busy working on a murder case for—of all people—Rebecca Mayfield. God, but that woman was a thorn in her side.

And it wasn't even Taylor Redmun's murder he was working on.

She phoned him. He sounded really busy, so they planned to meet later. Her information about Bridezilla could wait until they were face-to-face. She knew he'd be irritated that she and Richie had gone off to talk to anyone about it, and it might be better to break that news to him other than over the phone.

She told herself to relax. This was the life she'd chosen. To be the wife of a homicide inspector meant that her husband's hours would be crazy, that they'd make plans but if someone was murdered, Paavo might well need to cancel those plans. His work, his cases, and the need to catch the killer so that the victim would have justice, would always be a priority for him.

That's what made him who he was, and what made him the man she loved.

At times, she could hardly believe that after so much time being in love with Paavo and knowing he was worried about marrying her—worrying that he wasn't right for her, that she had led a life that had made her too spoiled and too pampered to ever put up with his hours, his cases, and his bad moods when the cases were going nowhere and he felt unequal to the task of solving them—that their wedding day was almost here.

To his surprise, and frankly to hers, a number of things happened that showed him just how tough she could be, including her saving his life more than once. He had finally come to believe the two of them were meant for each other, were meant to be together, and that he needed her in his life—maybe even as much as she needed him in hers.

She was feeling a little better about the chance of having her wedding reception at La Belle Maison, but decided to continue to attempt to find a back-up location. She knew her sisters were working on finding one as well, but so far they were having no luck.

She was about to try a third location, this one all the way out in Fairfax in Marin County—she was truly desperate—when her phone rang.

It was Wholly Matrimony, her caterer's business. She had put in a call to Chef Maurice to let him know they might have a change in venue, and had expected him to call her earlier that day. But, better late than never, as they say.

"Hello!" she said in her most cheery voice.

"Miss Amalfi?" It wasn't Chef Maurice, but a woman.

"Yes."

"This is Linda Withers. I'm Chef Maurice's assistant and business manager." Something about the tone of the woman's voice gave Angie a bad feeling deep in the pit of her stomach. "I'm afraid I have some terrible news."

No, no, no! Angie thought, but only spoke a very soft, "Yes?"

After a moment, Ms. Withers continued. "I'm sorry to say, Chef Maurice isn't here. I don't think he'll return by tomorrow night for your dinner on the cruise."

When she stopped speaking, Angie croaked out, "But he'll be back for Saturday's reception dinner."

"Well ..."

"*What are you trying to tell me? Of course, he'll be back! I have three-hundred people expecting to eat a fancy French meal! Where the hell is he?*"

"Miss Amalfi, I'm sorry. The truth is, we don't know where he is."

"You don't know? You mean he's missing? Have you contacted Missing Persons? The press? Put out an Amber Alert or whatever it is they do when an adult is missing? What have you done to find him? I'll call my fiancé. He'll get the right people to help you. This is terrible! He might be in awful danger."

"Wait, please, it's not what you're thinking." Angie heard her sniffle and then draw in her breath. "You see, our business hasn't been doing very well. We have creditors. Lots of them. We don't have the customer base we once did as more and more young people are going for all kinds of strange foods these days—raw, vegan, tofu-laced—not good, rich, calorie-filled, sauce-enhanced French cuisine. As a result, I think, I mean, it's just a guess mind you, but it's a good guess ..."

A sinking feeling struck; Angie feared she knew where this was going. "Out with it."

"He's absconded with what little money we had left. He disappeared. I think the check your father gave him to pay for the reception dinner—I mean, a fancy French meal plus wines for three hundred people, not to mention the Friday night meal—was simply too much temptation. He took the money and ran."

"*No!*"

"So it appears."

Angie suddenly felt so dizzy she feared she'd topple off the sofa. "But you've worked with him," she croaked. "You know how to cook his meals. And your kitchen staff is still there to help. You can put on the dinner. It might not be as perfect as Chef Maurice would have made it, but it'll be delicious, I'm sure."

"You haven't quite understood everything I've said." Withers sounded on the verge of tears. "We have no money left. No money to pay me or the staff for the work we've already done last week for a different wedding reception. No money to buy the food or the wine, let alone to pay for the time of the sous chefs, dishwashers, waiters or anything else."

"You've got my father's money!" Angie wailed. "You can't do this to me."

"I'm so sorry." Withers sounded as if her heart was broken. "But as of today, there's no longer any such thing as Wholly Matrimony."

Angie tried phoning the Never Sea-Sick Cruise and Events Charter, but kept getting an answering machine. Finally, desperate, she went down to the pier where the cruise boats were kept. She found the office, a small, one story, flat-roofed building. The door to it was locked.

She looked around, and then watched as a boat sailed away with a group of happy people on it.

Tomorrow night, her and her wedding party would sail off that way—thank God! At least charter boats were stable in this crazy world. Ironically, they made some people sea-sick.

And then, as she suspected might be the case, once the boat left the pier, a man and woman walked towards the office.

Angie ran up to them, explained who she was and that they needed to talk. One of them was Jessica Lenz, the cruise director she had spoken to on the phone a number of times. Jessica invited her inside.

The interior of the small building was decorated to look like the interior of a cabin cruiser, with wood paneling on the walls and ceiling, wooden planks on the floor, and a stuffed and mounted swordfish, ropes, tackle, and ocean scene artwork filling the walls.

"I know I told you that I didn't need your company to cater my dinner tomorrow night," Angie said, as they sat in

Jessica's office. "But something terrible has happened."

"Sorry to hear that." The director's words were brusque. She was a large woman, fair, with a drooping eye and her whitish blond hair pulled into a ponytail. She looked and sounded irritated.

"Yes." Angie gulped. "Well, you see, the company I had hired to cater the dinner seems to have folded. They aren't available."

Jessica's pale eyebrows lifted.

"I'm going to have thirty people at the dinner." Angie's voice rose higher. "Thirty hungry people. I was hoping your staff could help."

"My staff? On a Friday night?" She all but laughed. "We told everyone involved with food preparation that they wouldn't be needed. I know a number of them, if not all, have found other jobs. And to prepare a special meal, which I expect you want, requires time."

"I know, but I'm desperate. I need to feed them something. Anything!"

Jessica folded her arms, and thought a long moment. "I could try, but I warn you, it would only be a skeleton crew, and probably not our best people. The only thing we could serve on such short notice is roasted chicken."

"Chicken?" Visions of typical big dinner rubber chicken flashed across Angie's mind. "Please, something else."

"And, even serving chicken, there'll have to be a twenty-percent surcharge for the extra work of trying to find people who can roast the chicken, and serve with it mashed potatoes and succotash."

"Succo—" Angie was hyperventilating too much to finish the word. She hated the nasty little lima beans and flavorless everything else in succotash. This was a disaster, a complete disaster. If Chef Maurice hadn't vanished, she would murder him for what he was doing to her wedding.

"Can we work out something—"

"Take it or leave it. I mean, it'll be all I can do to find people to serve and know how to do more than boil water."

Angie shut her eyes, and tried to think.

"Well, if you don't want that, you can always buy thirty Happy Meals." At that, Jessica burst into laughter.

Angie gaped. What was wrong with the woman? She was tempted to walk out and tell her where she could put the thirty Happy Meals. But instead she swallowed her pride and her good taste, and said, "I'll take it."

Benny Simms watched the attractive, petite woman walk towards her Mercedes. Once he had her name, it was easy to use the Internet to find where she lived. She was even kind enough to post some pictures outside her apartment on Facebook. He was there, sitting in his 1988 Toyota, looking at her building and trying to think of how to get inside her apartment, when who should come zipping out of the garage in a shiny new Mercedes, but Angelina Amalfi herself.

He followed her.

She drove as if she were a woman possessed, and then

stood alone on a pier, clearly unhappy until she and a Valkyrie went into the office.

He got out of his car and waited behind a telephone pole for her to return to her Mercedes. This, he thought, was a good time and place to grab her, to put her out of her wedding-induced misery. He reached back to touch the hilt of the knife he had stuck in his back pocket.

Finally, he saw her. She walked fiercely, with purpose. He loved seeing her that way—her fire, her passion. He saw her take out a remote and click it to unlock the driver's door and even to start the engine. That was when he knew he had to hurry. He quickly realized she wasn't one to spend time looking in her visor's vanity mirror to check her make-up, or to carefully fasten her seatbelt so as not to wrinkle her clothes, or to do heaven only knew what else many women did, all the while leaving their driver's side door wide open.

In fact, as he neared, she was already in the car and grasping the handle to shut the door.

He reached out to stop it from closing. But she was stronger than he thought. Without missing a beat, she pulled hard and the door swung shut.

The tips of his first and second fingers got caught between the door and the frame of the car as it closed. He managed to yank them free before they became a bloody, flattened mess. They hurt like hell nonetheless as tears coursed down his unshaven cheeks.

He stood dumbfounded, his two fingers in his mouth as, oblivious to him, to his cry of pain, to the fact that he was standing right next to her car, she took off like a shot.

What could she possibly have been thinking about?

Chapter 9

Eight o'clock at night Homicide was empty except for Rebecca going through her computer to compare the stories told to her by members of the Redmun-Blythe wedding party. She heard footsteps on the tile floor and looked up.

Richie Amalfi strutted into the room. He always strutted or swaggered or sauntered. She hated that.

"I thought I'd find you here," he said with a smile.

This means trouble, she thought, but also noticed that he looked good. Damn good. She hated that reaction to him. The other inspectors in Homicide warned her to stay away from him. He wasn't to be trusted, they said. He could be into something illegal, they said. Even Paavo admitted he didn't really know what to make of Angie's cousin.

"Could this day get any worse?" she asked, frowning heavily. "Why, yes. It just did. What brings you here, Richie?"

His smile broadened as he sat down by her desk. "Rebecca Rulebook. You do know how to charm." He turned his phone towards her and showed a photo of Angie sitting in a bar. "I came to show you this."

"What's that supposed to mean?" she asked. She also hated

when he called her Rebecca Rulebook. What did she like about him? Hmm ... nothing.

"Not Angie, the woman behind her. Yolanda Herrera. She was friends with Taylor Redmun. They worked together at the Blue Velvet Pub on Columbus. She had a lot to say to us."

Outraged, Rebecca stood. *"You went nosing around my murder investigation?"*

He took her hand and tugged on it as if to pull her down to her chair again. Despite everything, something about his touch stirred her.

"Sit." His voice was smooth as warm butter. She pulled her hand free and continued to glare at him.

"I wasn't nosing around anything." He leaned back in the chair. "I was talking to Angie and learned she knows a guy who knew Taylor and Yolanda. She wanted to talk to Yolanda so, being a good cousin, I went along. Who knew what she might be walking into? And I knew that if she found out anything, it wasn't too likely she'd come visit you with the news."

His eyes were dark, his lids heavy, and for some reason she couldn't fathom, they always drew her in. She sucked in her breath and sat down once again in her chair. "So, what's this news you brought me? I take it I'm supposed to be overjoyed, right?"

He smirked. "You just might be."

She would have loved to wipe that smirk right off his face.

"Taylor liked to put on airs," he began. "But she was going nowhere but downhill, and fast. She liked snorting coke, even lost her job at the Blue Velvet because of it. But then she met

Leland Blythe—steady job, nice guy, and absolutely head over heels that a woman who looked like Taylor, and with dreams of becoming a movie star, should have any interest in him whatsoever. She wanted to move in with him, to let him support her. But to her amazement, he actually wanted to marry her."

"So she found a sap, big deal." Rebecca folded her arms, still managing to frown at him.

"Around the same time, she heard about a part in a movie being filmed in the city, and looked into it. It's apparently some cheap-ass, half sci-fi, half soft-porn thing about horny steel-eating creatures from outer space. To her, it was the next Star Wars. She got herself a small part—about three lines with lots of screaming and showing lots of skin—but then she heard a bigger role was opening up. That was when she decided to throw a wedding that would impress the people putting on the movie, the producer, director, and all the money men.

"She got Leland to agree to put up the money for La Belle Maison. Keep in mind, he doesn't have that much either, but he'd do anything for her. He was afraid if he said no, she'd walk. So he said yes, even though it nearly wiped out all his savings."

"Unbelievable," Rebecca murmured. No wonder no one liked the woman.

"But true. I had my cell phone on record as Angie and I talked to Yolanda. I'll email a copy to you. There's a lot of background noise, and lots of extra chatter like you've got to do to get people to open up and tell you what they really think. But I'm giving you the gist of our thirty or forty minute conversation."

"You got her to talk that long?"

"Sure. It was easy. The Blue Velvet wasn't that busy. And, she liked talking to me."

Rebecca's jaw tightened. There was something about Richie that, even when he was being helpful, rubbed her the wrong way.

But, maddeningly, there were other times ...

"Okay," she said, trying to keep her mind off the man, and concentrating on the helpful information he'd found out. "Send me the recording and I'll look into it."

"Hold it," he said. "You haven't heard the best part."

He said nothing until she lifted one eyebrow. That was as much as she'd ease up to let him know she was interested. It did the trick, and he continued, "After she did that, booked the big space, invited about fifty important people from the film, only ten showed up. The other guests were all Leland's family and friends. She didn't even invite Yolanda, her supposed best friend, even though Taylor had confided in her all along about everything."

Rebecca just shook her head at the complicated lives some people lived—and died living.

"Also, Yolanda said that the women Taylor asked to be her bridesmaids weren't asked because they were her friends. They weren't. They were chosen because they weren't very good looking, and that way Taylor would look even prettier."

"What a bitch!" Rebecca shouldn't have said that about her victim, but she couldn't hold it in any longer.

Professionalism be damned.

"Exactly," Richie said.

"So ..." Rebecca drew in her breath. "If all this is true, and I'm not saying it is or isn't at this point, then it's very likely not the bridesmaids or filmdom guests I should concentrate on, but maybe I need to look more closely at Leland's family and friends—and maybe at Leland himself." She faced her computer again. "I should get back to this."

Richie nodded, then stood. "Have you had your dinner yet?"

"I'm not hungry." She started to scroll through some information on the computer.

"You've got to eat. Come on. We can get something fast— even eat in the car, if you'd like."

She shook her head. "No, really."

"Okay," he said. "Well, I should get down to the club, make sure it's running okay, and I should let you finish up so you can get home before the sun comes up. Will I see you Saturday?"

She barely glanced up at him. "Saturday?"

"Paavo's wedding."

She turned back to the computer. "I don't think so. I'm not one for weddings. I'll probably still be working on this case. Hopefully wrapping it up."

"Rebecca," he said, his voice a deep rumble.

She did look up at him this time.

Dark eyes met hers and held a long moment; he wasn't smiling, but looking very serious. "The wedding is at three p.m.

I'm in the wedding party and have to get there early or I'd pick you up myself. Saints Peter and Paul's. Be there."

As she watched him head for the elevator, she knew she should have called out to tell him she wasn't going. But for some reason, she didn't.

Chapter 10

That morning, Angie felt as if she'd been run over by a train after the twin disasters of Chef Maurice absconding with the money for her reception and then having to serve her Friday night wedding party chicken and succotash. She hoped it wasn't an omen for Saturday's meal. The only thing not mucked up, so far, was that she would still have her beautiful wedding cake, assuming the bakery didn't burn down, which at this point was a distinct possibility.

The only bright spot in her dismal existence was that Paavo made it to her apartment last night around ten p.m. He told her that he and Yosh were 99.9% certain they knew who the murderer was in the case they were working, and were on the trail of evidence to prove it.

When she switched the conversation to the Taylor Redmun-Blythe murder investigation, things weren't progressing as favorably. She told him how she and Cousin Richie met with Taylor's supposed best friend, Yolanda Herrera, and all she'd learned. Before lecturing her about the dangers of talking to anyone involved in a murder case, Paavo called Rebecca Mayfield to fill her in. But he learned Richie had already been there.

Fortunately, after his conversation with Rebecca, Paavo didn't bother with his usual warnings about Angie not getting involved in Homicide's cases. She was glad. Lectures were the last thing she wanted from him.

He left at 6 a.m. to go home, shower, and report to work.

Angie saw him off, then went back to bed and tried, unsuccessfully, to go back to sleep. Brides needed their "beauty rest," after all. Finally, she gave up. She got up, put on the coffee, and then wearily opened the apartment door to get the morning *San Francisco Chronicle.* The newspaper delivery man didn't bring it all the way to the penthouse for her, but since her father owned the building, the doorman saw that it reached her apartment door each day.

She stepped back inside, took the rubber band off the paper, and unfolded it as she stumbled towards the kitchen for her coffee.

The headlines screamed "Never Sea-sick Cruise & Events Charter Company Busted!"

"*Nooooo!*" Angie screamed even louder than the headlines.

On shaky legs she carried the newspaper to her petit-point living room sofa and sat with a thud as she read the article.

Narcotics officers from the DEA had conducted an undercover sting operation and found that several employees were involved in illegal smuggling of heroin. The DEA had no idea how far the smuggling went, or if the owners of the charter boats were involved or not. As a precaution, at ten p.m. last night they raided the company offices and shut down the entire operation. It would remain closed while their investigation was conducted.

Angie had had little sleep, no morning coffee, and now this. She phoned Never Sea-Sick Cruises to find out what was going on. Would the ship she had rented still sail that evening? Would her guests still be served rubber-chicken?

Not only did no one answer, she didn't even get the answering machine.

She suddenly found herself in a fetal position on her couch, whimpering softly.

Finally, unable to stomach her own self-pity, she called her mother. Even if her sisters weren't answering her calls, her mother was. Serefina told her to come to her house in one hour.

Having no idea what else to do, she decided to listen to her mother.

To her surprise, her sisters were there when she arrived.

One look at all of them, and she burst into tears. "I can't do it," she cried. "I give up. My wedding is a complete failure. We'll have the marriage ceremony, thank everyone for attending, and then send them all home. We'll get an early start for our honeymoon. Unless a typhoon hits Hawaii. Maybe I'll drown in it and put an end to my misery."

Serefina, who was somewhat chubby and had a penchant for polka dot dresses which only emphasized her roundness, gave her youngest daughter a long hug. Serefina then brought her into the kitchen and sat her at the table with a big cup of coffee and some iced Italian cookies. But at the moment, not even her mother's number one choice in comfort food helped. The coffee, however, did. Somewhat.

"We'll figure out something," Bianca said. Bianca, Angie's oldest sister, was the matronly one, with little make-up and straight chin-length dark brown hair. Bianca had practically raised Angie before the family had much money, when Serefina used to work nearly as many hours as Salvatore at his shoe store, and all his profits were plowed into more stores and San Francisco real estate.

"No." Angie shook her head, then took a deep breath, shoulders squared and head high as she proclaimed, "I know when I'm defeated. I've tried everything. This is a disaster. That's the specialty my wedding day will be known for—the reception that wasn't. And the rehearsal dinner that also wasn't. Neither on land nor sea can I feed people. None of it will happen. From this hour forward, I will try no more. I give up."

"Don't be silly. We'll work it out," Caterina insisted. Called "Cat," Angie's second oldest sister was everything opposite from the plain, motherly Bianca. Cat kept her weight so low her shape was more like an ironing board than a woman, and her dark hair had been bleached within an inch of its life to an ash blonde color. She also had a husband and a son she spent little time with. "I was reading just the other day how there was a tornado in Kansas that destroyed a wedding chapel. And, in Chicago, a toy drone flew through an outdoor wedding ceremony and scared all the guests so badly they stampeded to get away from it. Then, the food served at a wedding in Florida spoiled and caused everyone to get sick to their stomachs."

Job's comforters would love Caterina, Angie thought, but made no comment.

"So don't you dare give up," Cat added. "It could be a lot worse."

"I don't have a choice," Angie said.

"We always have choices in life," intoned Maria as she pressed her fingertips together like some om-chanting guru. Maria was Angie's most exotic sister, always adorned with silver and turquoise jewelry and having long black hair that reached nearly to her waist—and also her most "spiritual." If Maria started in with words about searching for the right path and doing whatever was "best" in life even if it wasn't necessarily what one most wanted to do, Angie was sure she'd slug her. Angie was a God-loving, God-fearing Catholic, and she loved her sister, but Maria's holier-than-thou attitude sometimes pushed her over the edge.

Spare me, please, Angie thought, but kept her mouth shut.

"It tore at my heart," Maria said, "reading of how, in Bangladesh, a pack of wild dogs ran through a wedding party and made off with all the food. The wedding may have been ruined, but the hungry dogs were able to eat, so it was good after all. Your problems are nothing compared to the troubles in less fortunate parts of the world."

Angie held her head in her hands and ground her teeth.

Frannie looked at her sisters with disgust. Frannie was nearest to Angie in age, which was probably why she and Angie were the least close of the sisters. Angie remembered far too well how Frannie used to steal her toys and pinch her arm when their parents weren't watching. "There are no wild dogs or tornadoes in San Francisco, Angie's wedding is indoors, and the food ... well, nobody has to worry about it spoiling."

"Very funny," Angie muttered.

"Remember Angie," Frannie continued, "Seth and I had a very simple wedding ceremony."

And look at how well that turned out, Angie thought, but again didn't say anything. Seth and Frannie's marriage was notoriously fraught.

"Look on the bright side," Bianca said. "If all this had to happen, at least it happened before Saturday. We have time to come up with a decent wedding reception for you."

"Aaaarrrgh," Angie wailed. Sometimes her oldest sister's eternally optimistic nature was nauseating. "All I wanted was one special day. That's all. Was that really too much to ask?"

"What's important is that the two of you get married," Serefina said. "Not all the frills that go along with it."

"But it's my wedding day!"

Serefina just shook her head. "*Capisco*. Okay, we'll see what we can do."

One by one her sisters hugged her and left the house. Only after they were gone did Angie sit down with her head on her mother's shoulder and let the tears flow. Serefina put her arms around her youngest daughter and thought.

Chapter 11

Friday, Noon – 1 day, 3 hours before the wedding

"You've got to hear these kids," Yosh said as Paavo watched him lead two teenage boys in his direction. They both wore baseball caps backwards, baggy pants, baggy sweatshirts, and holey tennis shoes.

Yesterday, through the afternoon and into the night, the two inspectors had managed to speak to all the tenants in the apartment building where the bride's body was found. Not one of them admitted to seeing anything or anyone strange in the building, and no one claimed to have reported anything to the building manager. Both those statements confirmed Paavo and Yosh's working theory about the case. But they still had no physical evidence.

The inspectors decided to spend this day talking to people who lived in neighboring flats and apartments.

The medical examiner had succeeded in pulling fingerprints from the corpse. The woman's name was Shawnita Hickman, African-American, twenty-two years old.

Paavo quickly found a missing person's report filed on her in Los Angeles. He called the detective who had the case. The detective filled him in on the details.

Shawnita Hickman had been arrested several times in Los Angeles on drug charges, and was known to hang around with the "899" gang there. When last seen, she was on the way to her outdoor wedding in a park with Latrell Cruz, a gang member, when the two got into a fight. She slugged him, he slugged her back, and she ran off in her wedding dress. She was never seen again.

Her friends looked for her, but couldn't find her. Four days later, a sister went to the police and filed a missing person's report. The sister believed the 899s had killed Shawnita for dissing Latrell by leaving him at the altar, such as it was. The police investigated, but could find no evidence of a murder or anything else. Not that they tried particularly hard, and not that the people they interviewed were particularly cooperative. The LAPD concluded that Shawnita must have realized her life was in danger and had run away. They assumed she would eventually be picked up on another drug arrest, and that's how they'd find her. That was usually the way these cases went, the detective said. But that "next drug arrest" never came.

Shawnita's disappearance had taken place six months earlier, and the M.E. believed Shawnita had been dead at least six months.

Now, Yosh turned to the two teenagers. "Tell Inspector Smith what you told me."

The taller boy began. "I was curious about the black window in that apartment building." As he spoke, he pointed at the building where the body had been found. "So, I decided to see what it was hiding. I didn't want to steal nothing, just look, you know? So one night, I worked on pulling out the nails and then stuck a slim jim through the frame to open the lock. It took a while, but I did it."

The boy stopped then, and looked up at Yosh. "Go on," Yosh said. "You're not in trouble with us. Just tell the Inspector what you saw."

The boy bit his bottom lip, then spoke. "I looked inside. I saw ... I saw a woman dressed like a bride on the bed. It was creepy, so I shut the window and ran. I told my bro, but he didn't believe me. Also, it was night and the only light was from a street lamp near the window. I thought maybe I was wrong. Maybe it was just a dress, or some rags. Digs—that's my bro here—said he wanted to see her, so we went back the next day." At that, the shorter boy nodded in agreement.

"Then what?" Paavo urged.

The tall boy continued. "I pushed the window open and we was gonna try to squeeze through and go inside, but we saw that the light in the room was on. And then we saw the woman. It was like I thought. She was dressed in white and had a veil around her head—like a bride. But her face was all squashed and ugly. I never seen any face so bad, man. And she wasn't alone. A guy was laying on the bed with her."

"A guy," Paavo repeated. "Do you know who he is?"

The boys nodded. "He's the white guy lives in the building. Not too old, brown hair, kind of small."

Paavo met Yosh's gaze. "Simms," he said.

"We knew it." Yosh smiled.

Paavo took out his notebook, reviewed the information

he'd gotten when he talked to Benny Simms, then phoned Evelyn Ramirez. She was in her office.

After explaining which case he was calling about, he said, "You found some cloth fibers in the victim's throat. Could you see if those fibers match material used in a 1988 Toyota Corona?"

She said she'd call back soon. Paavo and Yosh took more detail from the boys, including their full names and where they lived. They didn't want to use the young boys' testimony, but hoped to use the information to find physical evidence of Simms' guilt.

In a few minutes, Ramirez called back. "The fibers match material Toyota used in the trunk compartments of their cars back in the 1980s."

Paavo nodded at Yosh. "Got him."

"Oh, one more thing," Ramirez said. "We were able to pull some DNA off the corpse, and I'm certain it came from the killer. The lab's backed up, but we should have those results in about a week for you."

"Good. What kind of DNA?"

"Let's just say the sick bastard went in for necrophilia. A whole lot, from the looks of it." With that, she hung up.

Paavo shook his head at the image her words caused. Now, he just needed to find Simms to make the arrest.

Chapter 12

It only took a couple of hours before Maria, of all people, found a space for Angie's rehearsal dinner that very night. Maria might talk and act like a nun on a good day, but her husband was a dashing, formerly wild-living jazz musician, Dominic Klee. One of his biggest fans was the owner of the 100 Lusk Street Restaurant, a trendy place near the Giants Ballpark. It had a private dining room that could fit up to forty people, and he was able to make it available to Angie's wedding party.

As Maria gave her the news, Angie was speechless. The restaurant was beautiful. It might not be as much fun as cruising San Francisco Bay might have been, but at this point, its ambiance and the quality of its food was much more than she'd imagined being able to find.

Now, if only she could find a caterer to prepare the dinner for her wedding reception, and if she could get La Belle Maison turned over to her on time, all would be well once more. She had dreamed of having a "La Belle Maison wedding reception" for a long, long time.

She was making phone calls trying to find a caterer, but

soon realized that her sisters had already made contact with every place she called. Not only was she getting nowhere, she was irritating people, several of whom snapped, "I already told you I was busy!"

Finally, she stopped, and sat back on her sofa.

Her nerves were completely frayed, she was falling apart, and felt nothing but anxiety and disappointment on the day before what should have been the happiest day of her life.

But she knew one place that could repair her mood.

She got into her car and drove to the house she and Paavo would soon call home. She loved her apartment, but even more, she loved the house that they had found and were buying.

It did, however, have a controversial history. A young couple who had owned it some thirty years earlier had been murdered there. The house had been a rental for a while, but when renters learned of the murders, most quickly moved. As a result, it had stood empty for years.

Normally, that sort of history was a deal breaker in real estate. Who would want to live in a home where someone had been murdered? But, when one of the potential buyers was a homicide detective, the thought of a dead body or two wasn't all that scary. Besides, the young couple had been killed outdoors, not inside the house.

There were also rumors that the house was haunted. Of course, Angie didn't believe in ghosts, and neither did Paavo, but he did want to be sure Angie loved the place and would feel comfortable living there. To her surprise, not only did the potential "ghostly" nature of the house not bother her, it made her feel safe and welcome.

She had no idea why because, as she explained to Paavo, she didn't believe in ghosts.

Bottom line, because of murders and spiritual innuendos, she and Paavo got a fantastic deal on the place. They were able to buy a much more beautiful home in a much more sensational setting than she ever dreamed possible. Number 51 Clover Lane was in one of San Francisco's prime locations, just off Sea Cliff Avenue and overlooking the Pacific Ocean. The down-payment came from the sale of Paavo's small home in the Richmond district. Murder and ghost-free as it was, it brought an excellent price because of its location and the fact that Google and Twitter employees were flooding San Francisco with so much money that they didn't much care what they bought since they had enough money to do a complete renovation or even a tear-down.

Paavo found such a buyer only one day after the house was offered for sale. He built into the negotiations being able to continue to live in the home until the week after the wedding.

For the mortgage, they got a loan at the bank where the father of Angie's long-time neighbor and good friend, Stanfield Bonnette, was president.

As Paavo put it, for the first time ever, he found a reason to like Stan Bonnette. Angie had to chuckle at that. Paavo wasn't jealous of Stan—no one would be—but he knew that Stan was forever suggesting Angie drop Paavo and marry him. Not that Stan was in love with her; he was in love with her *cooking*.

The day after their wedding, Mr. and Mrs. Smith would fly to a honeymoon cottage far off the beaten path in Kauai. All Angie wanted was a place with no telephones, no crime, and where no one would interrupt their honeymoon. For once in her life, she wanted Paavo all to herself. She could hardly wait.

They would spend a week there. When they returned, they would go to their new house. It was already furnished with a quite a few things, such as the new master bedroom set with a California king-size bed. Her queen-sized one, a bed she must admit had served her and Paavo well, would be relegated to the guest room.

The day following that, the movers would pick up all her possessions plus Paavo's few belongings from his house—which he would then turn over to the new owners—and deliver everything to Clover Street.

And so she headed for her soon-to-be home. She wanted to just sit for a while and try not stress over the disaster her Big Day had become. Even before this latest string of disasters, the house had come to feel like a talisman to her as the pressures of the wedding mounted.

As soon as she walked in the front door and opened the living room drapes, she began to feel more at peace.

A week earlier she had bought an automatic espresso maker for the house—a wedding present to herself and Paavo. She set it up and made herself an Americano, then took the drink into the living room where she'd put a couple of folding director's chairs and a little plastic table—all items that would probably end up out on the deck or in a closet when her "real" furniture arrived.

The windows overlooked a deck and small lawn area that led to a back fence. Beyond it were a few cypress trees and then a cliff that dropped to China Beach. She couldn't see the cliff. All she saw past her fence, past the trees, was the ocean. When all was quiet, with the sliding glass doors or windows open, she could hear the gentle murmur of waves meeting the shore far below.

On a clear day, she could see the Farallon Islands out in the water, chunks of weathered rock that were no more than landing and nesting spots for seabirds, seals, and sea lions. It also had an automated lighthouse, and, she'd heard, a gazillion mice. The islands weren't open to the public.

As she sat, she turned away from the windows to stare at the walls and try to decide what color she should have them painted. They were all off white at the moment, and she'd like a little more warmth.

Movement in the backyard caught her eye. The four-legged visitor who had come to call several times before, a little white "Scottie" dog—a West Highland Terrier she believed it was—sat at the sliding glass door and looked in at her.

"Hello, again," she said as she opened the door. He ran inside and straight to the kitchen where, he'd learned, she kept a supply of dog food. He was a strange little creature. Whenever she tried to pet him, he ran from her, but at the same time, he seemed to enjoy sitting and watching at her. She would have loved to pick him up or at least pet him, but if he didn't want to be touched, she wasn't going to force herself on him and scare him away.

He seemed well cared for, but she had no idea where he lived. She had asked neighbors if they knew where his home was, but none had ever seen him, which struck her as odd.

She did know, however, that the couple who had been murdered on the grounds had owned this type of dog. She wondered if the one she saw was a descendant of that dog, and this one had some kind of doggie ESP that caused him to come and visit. Since he was out in the yard each time she visited, she knew his home had to be nearby. For sure, with his coat shiny and mat-free, and looking well-fed and healthy even as he came to the house and begged for food, he was no stray.

She opened a can of Castor & Pollux Organic dog food for him. Never having owned a dog, when she went shopping for dog food, she bought what sounded, basically, good enough to eat.

He wagged his little tail as she dished out a half can—that was as much as he ever ate at one sitting—and put the cute porcelain doggy bowl she bought for him on the floor along with a bowl of fresh water. He waited until she backed away, then ran over and daintily ate.

When he finished, he drank some water, and then went into the living room to lie down on the carpet, his front paws crossed, and expectantly watched her. Unfortunately, she had no idea what he was watching her *for*.

Angie loved to talk, and so she talked to him about her upcoming nuptials, the problems she was having, and even her ideas about painting and otherwise remodeling the house.

As she kept talking, he placed his head down atop his paws and watched her every movement, every wave of her hands, with his big, brown eyes. He seemed to follow her every word. Suddenly, to her surprise, he growled and trotted over to the sliding glass door.

When she opened it, he barked and raced across the lawn.

Serefina Amalfi made herself a cup of coffee and then ate the cookies her daughters didn't touch as she sat at the kitchen table and tried to think of what to do about Angie's reception. Her heart ached to see her daughter so unhappy the day before her wedding. She wished Angie could understand that what made a wedding wasn't all the surrounding falderal—she loved the word that was close to *fardello* in Italian which meant "baggage"—but it was the happiness of two people in love deciding to spend their lives together, and even about the children, God willing, who might come to be as a result of that union.

But she also recognized that as the bride who had planned and looked forward to her wedding day for such a long time, Angie couldn't help but feel horribly disappointed that all the plans she and her sisters had developed were turning to nothing before her very eyes.

Still, a part of Serefina didn't like the idea at all of her youngest daughter, her baby, having her reception in the hall where the last bride had been murdered. It was bad enough Angie was marrying a cop. Serefina had seen first-hand the danger his job caused him, and saw how Angie couldn't stay clear of much of that danger herself.

Even worse, the two *testa-dura*'s wouldn't listen to reason and bought a house where the prior owners had been murdered. *Madonna mia!* She didn't care how beautiful the house was, there was no way on this earth she would live where someone had died.

She'd never understand her daughter.

At least now, without her needing to say a word, she had the chance to do something about Angie's wedding reception. To make it wonderful.

It seemed to her, all this bad luck meant someone had given her daughter the evil eye. Some jealous person, most likely, who didn't like seeing the Amalfi family happy. If she ever found out who was behind it, that person would pay. But the best revenge would be to pull off Angie's wedding and make it even better than it might otherwise have been.

And even if, as her daughters tried to tell her, there was no such thing as the evil eye, Serefina still hated the thought of trying to be happy and celebrating a wedding in a place filled with the specter of recent violent death circling about it.

Maybe ghosts and spirits were as imaginary as the evil eye, but why take chances?

Out of the blue, a plan came to her. The more she thought about it, the better it seemed. She started making phone calls. After she talked to her other four daughters, relatives, and a number of friends, it seemed she could pull it off. Now, she just had to talk to her husband.

Sal Amalfi had a bad heart. Presenting him with the bills for Angie's wedding had been difficult until Serefina realized Sal's heart wasn't as delicate as she had feared because some of those bills would surely have given a weaker man cardiac arrest. But now she had to tell him that not only had he spent a fortune on the wedding reception, but it looked as if it wasn't going to happen. And, while they might get a bit of a refund on the venue, the money spent on the food, wine, and catering service was very likely gone for good.

But she had a solution. Sort of.

She had no idea what Angie would think of it. And the one person she didn't talk to that afternoon was Angie.

Chapter 13

Benny Simms boosted himself up onto the six-foot tall wooden fence at the back of the house Angie Amalfi had entered. He had been able to grab the top and pull himself high enough that he could see over it while pressing the rubber soles of his tennis shoes hard against the wood so he wouldn't slide back down. But he wondered if he had the arm strength to pull the rest of his body high enough to get his leg up to the top of the fence and then over it.

From where he hung, he couldn't see inside the house. He didn't know if she was alone or not.

If he could manage to climb over the fence and then inch closer to the house, he should be able to sneak up to a window and find out what the situation was.

Somehow, he had to find the strength to reach her. His bride.

And maybe she'd like him and be nice to him instead of screaming and trying to run from him the way Shawnita had done.

Poor Shawnita. All he had wanted to do was to help her, but the fist to the face that she'd received from her groom had made her go all woozy. Despite that, she had fought against him as he pulled her into the alley where he'd parked his car. He couldn't stop her cries until he banged her head against a wall a few times. After all, he didn't want the 899 killers to hear her and have them turn on him.

She slumped to the ground and stopped moving at all. She was still breathing, so he told himself she had decided to cooperate and stay quiet. But then he saw some 899ers nearing the alley. He put her in the trunk of his car and drove off before they paid any attention to him. He didn't stop until hours later when he needed gas.

When he was finally sure those gang-bangers weren't somehow following him, he pulled off the highway and opened the trunk. That was when he wondered if, in his fear and excitement earlier that afternoon, he'd hit her too hard.

Shawnita was dead.

He brought her back to San Francisco. After a few weeks of him doing all he could to keep the store room sealed off so the smell wouldn't get out, and to keep cleaning her body and using bug spray on it so the maggots and such wouldn't turn her skin to soup, the smell went away, and the insects died.

And finally, she was his, completely his, until those damn kids messed up everything. He thought about ignoring them, but he knew that eventually they'd tell what they saw and then the police would come nosing around. The best thing he could do was call the cops, and pretend he was the one who had discovered her.

Those stupid, stupid cops believed him. They believed he

knew nothing about who she was, or how she'd gotten there. Idiots! He smiled at his own cleverness.

But, he thought, an eye for an eye. Or in this case, a bride for a bride.

As he dangled from the fence, clutching the top of it and trying, but failing, to boost himself up, the woman opened the sliding glass door. He stopped moving to gape at her, to admire her beauty. He watched as she looked down at her feet, and he heard her say, "Go on, boy! Go get 'im."

He nearly slipped off the fence, so confused was he, wondering who or what she was talking to when he felt something bang against his leg. He looked down, but saw nothing until the jeans material just above his tennis shoes suddenly jerked outward, away from his leg and began to wriggle from side to side as if something had grabbed it and was pulling on it—as if something wanted to pull him off the fence. But nothing was there.

He watched as a small rip appeared in the denim. It looked as if made by a knife ... or a tooth. His heart nearly stopped. He lost his grip, and fell onto the ground, landing on his backside.

He still saw nothing, but he had felt something ... he thought.

What was going on? What was wrong with him?

He got to his feet and told himself he was imagining things. It was probably a nail or something left in the wood that had snagged his jeans. He was going to try to climb back up on the fence when out of the blue he saw a little white dog sitting on the ground between him and the street. He didn't know where it had come from, and hadn't heard it approach.

Something, he decided, was really, really wrong. He looked around. The dog's cold brown eyes stared hard at him. A chill rippled down his back. He really wanted to go get his bride, but something told him not to. Not now, in any case. *I can return another day. Or even later today. No problem.*

It was just a little dog, and yet something about it scared him. He backed away from the fence even as he smiled at the tiny beast. "Nice doggie-doggie. Good boy. That's a good, good boy."

Paavo's gut gave him a very bad feeling when he got a call from the uniform responding to the APB on Benny Simms' car. Fortunately, there weren't many yellow 1988 Toyota Coronas with dents in both front fenders still on the road in San Francisco. The car was spotted in the tony Sea Cliff, which was the land of BMWs, Mercedes, and even a Tesla or two or twenty. Not junks. It stood out like a sore thumb.

His nerves got even worse when he heard the car's location—only a block from Clover Street. He immediately called Angie's cell phone, but got no answer. *It can't be. Not Angie; please, God, not Angie.*

She often didn't hear her phone, he reminded himself. If she was out, she buried it in a big leather purse with lots of other junk, and with noise around her ....

Or she might have simply turned off the ringer, depending on where she was, or if she wanted to take a nap, since he knew she hadn't slept well at all last night. It probably meant nothing.

But it wouldn't be the first time some sick-o decided to go after friends, relatives, co-workers, lovers, of the person he thought was persecuting him. Knowing what he did about Simms and the corpse, maybe Simms thought of the body as his "bride," and wanted another. Who better than the bride of the person who took his away?

Sometimes Paavo really hated his job.

"You don't think ..." Yosh couldn't finish his thought as he realized Paavo was speeding up.

"Why not?" Paavo said. "An attractive bride-to-be. She's alone, distracted, kindly ... even to strangers." He couldn't go on.

"She might not be at your new house," Yosh said.

"True," Paavo said. "Or, she might be."

Paavo didn't go looking for Simms' car. He went straight to his house. His heart sank when he saw Angie's car in the driveway. No other car was around.

As they got out, a man walking a black standard poodle on a leash came running towards them. "Do you have a cell phone on you?" he cried. "Someone's got to call the police!"

"We are the police," Paavo said, pushing aside his jacket to show his badge. "What's wrong?"

"A body, a man ... he's at the foot of the cliff, down on China Beach. I imagine he must have fallen. He's not moving, and there seems to be a lot of blood. I'm no good at climbing, so I didn't—"

He stopped talking because both Paavo and Yosh were running from him towards the edge of the cliff.

Paavo peered over it. The body was face down, but its size, the hair color and length, were those of Benny Simms. And the clothes were the same as Simms wore while being questioned. A pool of blood had formed under the man's head.

Paavo inched closer to see if anyone—any woman—had also fallen and was lying near him. Simms appeared to be alone. But why was he down there? What was he doing on the cliff?

Paavo looked back towards his and Angie's house and paled.

"I'll take it from here," Yosh said. "You go to the house. Make sure Angie's inside it and okay."

Paavo froze. Yosh put his hand on his shoulder. "She's all right. I know it. Go to her."

Paavo took a step, then another, and soon he was running.

He found his key and opened the front door. "Angie? Angie? Are you here?"

No answer.

"Angie?" he called as he ran into the kitchen. He saw her handbag on the counter—her cell phone with his urgent messages was most likely inside it.

He ran back to the living room, spun around, hand on the back of his neck, trying to think, then he moved towards the back yard.

She was sitting out on the deck.

She jumped at the sound of the sliding glass door opening and turned around. She looked surprised, but then gave him a big smile as she stood, the kind that lighted her eyes and brightened his days. "Paavo! What are you doing here?"

He could scarcely breathe as the feelings he had for this woman swept over him. He wanted to hold her, but he also didn't want to scare her—he didn't want her to even hear about anything ugly today of all days. "I was in the area and decided to drive by and check on the place. I was surprised to see your car. But what are *you* doing here?" he asked as he quickly crossed to her. Then, unable to stop himself, he put his arms around her and held her tight.

"Is everything all right?" she asked.

"Now, it is," he said, then kissed her, a long kiss filled with love.

She stepped back, slightly breathless. "Something has happened."

He grinned. "No, not at all. So, what are you up to? Why are you here?"

Since they had no outdoor furniture yet, they sat on the deck, their legs dangling off the side. It was only a couple of steps down to the lawn-covered yard.

"Sometimes," she began, "over the past few weeks and months when things like our wedding arrangements turned complicated, and I felt as if I couldn't make one more decision, I would come over here and remind myself of what's really important. There's something soothing about this house, about its location on this point of land where I can hear the steady, eternal sound of the ocean. And, of course, it has my little doggie friend." With that she stopped talking and looked around. "Hmm, he was just here with me. He must have run off when you opened the sliding glass door. Anyway, as I was saying, I've always felt welcomed here, as if it was a little haven. It sounds funny, but I feel protected."

"I didn't know that," he said, his arm around her shoulders. "But I'm glad you've told me. I was worried you'd feel isolated since I have to work nights so often. It's not like Stan is right next door."

"Hmm ... there's something I need to talk to you about," she said with a small grin. "That small house across the street is empty."

"No. He didn't."

"You never know about Stan."

"I'm glad you like him Angie, but to me, he's a pain in the—"

"I know. But he's got a good heart."

Paavo heard the wail of police sirens growing louder.

"All right, Paavo." Angie eyed him suspiciously. "What's really going on?"

"Someone found a body."

"Oh, no! A neighbor?"

"No. Just some drifter wandering through apparently. Nothing to worry about. But that's why Yosh and I were near. He's taking care of everything while I came to check on you."

Her eyebrows rose. "So that's why you looked so worried when you came in."

"Well ..."

"Paavo, haven't I told you that you don't have to worry

105

about me? I know how to take care of myself."

His gaze drank in each feature of her expressive face. "You're right. You do, and I know it, but I'll still always worry about you simply because I love you."

They held each other until Yosh came knocking at the door. Time to go.

Chapter 14

Friday, 9 p.m. – 18 hours before the wedding

Rebecca met with the crime scene inspectors to discuss their findings. They had lifted a number of fingerprints from La Belle Maison's kitchen and anteroom, but none matched any known criminals. The knife used to kill Taylor had plenty of smudged fingerprints that belonged to the kitchen staff, but no others. When CSI found a white cloth napkin under a table in the anteroom, they concluded the killer probably used it to pick up the murder weapon, thus smudging any fingerprints already on it.

They also believed the killer had to be a man, given the strength needed to penetrate Taylor Redmun-Blythe's back. Some women might be able to do it, but looking over the female guests and bridesmaids, most appeared—especially to Rebecca's eyes—to be in pathetically poor physical condition. Rebecca was proud that she did her best to spend at least three hours at the gym each week, plus close to an hour at the firing range.

The wedding had a still photographer, but at the key moment his back had been to the anteroom. Even worse, when he did notice the bride stumbling towards the cake, he had been so shocked he lowered his camera to watch.

Rebecca collected the photos taken by guests using smart phones. Since most of the guests weren't particularly close to the couple, few bothered to take any pictures except the movie people—but the photos they took were all of each other. Using them, however, she did find the "missing" third bridesmaid that Sally Lankowitz had mentioned. She was out on the deck smoking a cigarette.

Rebecca determined three people weren't in the photographer's last few photos, and weren't in those cell phone photos time-stamped near the time of the murder. The three were the groom, Leland Blythe; his brother, Mason Blythe; and his best man, Darrel Gruber.

Of the three, Leland supposedly loved the victim, Darrel clearly didn't care for her but he was a long-time friend of Leland's and seemed to want his friend to be happy, and Mason also didn't much like Taylor even though he supposedly hardly knew her. Actually, other than Leland, Rebecca couldn't find anyone who genuinely liked Taylor, so not being a fan hardly made a person a suspect.

Rebecca ran her fingers through her long hair, then held her head as she stared at her computer and the evidence before her. It was already Friday night, and she knew that if she couldn't turn La Belle Maison over to Paavo and his wedding by noon the next day, her name would be mud in Homicide. He and Yosh had already solved a case that might have been hers. Benny Simms, now deceased, was the man seen with the body of Shawnita Higgins. Although they might never be able to prove he had murdered her, the circumstantial evidence was strong enough to close the case.

But that didn't help Rebecca's case any. In fact, it made the lack of evidence she and Sutter were dealing with even worse. Everyone in Homicide was hoping to see the Taylor Redmun-Blythe case solved. Every one of them had been invited to Paavo's wedding, including Lieutenant Eastwood. To the surprise of all of them, the tight-ass boss granted the whole squad the afternoon off to attend the wedding and the reception. They had been looking forward to the dancing and some really good food—and to watching one of their own get married. But now, she stood in their way.

Even she was beginning to hate herself.

She was at her wits end, and, late though it was, she decided to interview the three men again, one by one.

That evening, the wedding rehearsal went off without a hitch, as Angie hoped it would. She was surprised that, after all the planning, the worry, and the recent disappointment, to be in the church with her family and wedding party surrounding her, holding hands with Paavo as they listened to the priest's instructions along with those of the office aide who helped with the more secular aspects of the ceremony, it all suddenly became more real to her than it had up to that point.

Before that, it was almost as if she had the starring role in a play, a performance. But now, it all became real life, a lifetime commitment in the eyes of God to the man she loved. Paavo wasn't Catholic, but he had attended marriage counseling classes with her at the church, and doing so, had come to appreciate the spiritual side of the union beyond the legalistic and civic. He even admitted, once, that he couldn't help but wish he could believe as deeply as she did—that he envied her her faith. She only smiled and nodded. Such words, she knew from watching others, could be an important first step.

After the surprisingly moving rehearsal, they went off for the rehearsal dinner at the restaurant Maria had found. The restaurant even let the large group order from the full menu, and somehow managed to serve them all close to the same time.

"If only everything would go as smoothly tomorrow," Angie said, as she stood with her parents and Paavo saying good-bye to friends and relatives.

"Somehow, it'll work out for you, sweetie," her best friend, Connie Rogers said as she gave her a big hug. Connie, who was divorced, would be Angie's matron of honor. "Haven't we always gotten out of one crazy situation after the other?"

Tears came to Angie's eyes as she hugged Connie back. "You can say that again. As long as you're with me, Connie, we'll make it work."

"And me," Stan said. Angie had talked Paavo into making Stan one of his groomsmen.

"And you!" Angie hugged him as well.

"I'll drop by tonight for a midnight snack," Stan said, wiping away a tear. "It'll be my last one in your apartment. I'll try not to cry on your trousseau."

"If you do, you'll be attending the wedding with black eyes," Angie warned. "I'll see you later."

Only her sisters and parents were left. "Tell her," Bianca said to their mother.

"Tell me what?" Angie asked.

Serefina glared at Bianca. "I didn't want to say anything, but we've got something worked out for you. If you can't have the reception you want, we've got a back-up plan."

"You do? Where? Who's the caterer?"

"Don't worry about it, Angelina!" Serefina said. "You just think about being a beautiful bride for your handsome groom." She faced Paavo. "*Caro mio,* you make me so happy. I look forward to dancing at your wedding, and I will."

"But, but—" Angie sputtered.

"*Andiamo!* Time for all of us to go home. We have a big day tomorrow."

"And tonight," Frannie muttered.

"Tonight?" Angie asked.

"Nothing," Frannie said quickly. "I just have to figure out what I'm going to wear tomorrow, that's all."

Angie wasn't sure she liked all this secrecy, but before she knew it, Paavo had her out the door, his arm around her, and she had more interesting things to think about.

Chapter 15

Richie showed up at Homicide at 9 a.m. Saturday morning, to find Rebecca all alone. She looked as if she'd been up all night.

"No luck?" he asked, putting a non-fat latte from Starbucks on her desk. He knew she liked them.

She looked surprised by the coffee. "Thanks," she murmured, then added, "No luck at all."

He could see she was exhausted and beyond frustrated. From what she'd told him about past cases, and what he'd heard from others, she'd never had one of these "locked room" type cases before. Always in the past, she'd go out and talk to people, search the crime scene, and if nothing turned up, she'd find more people to question, and would widen the scope of the search. In this case, from what friends on the force had told him, she'd talked to everyone, and CSI had gone over practically the entire building with a fine tooth comb. Security cameras around La Belle Maison proved that no one who wasn't a guest or employee had entered or left the venue throughout the day or night of the wedding, which meant that the killer was one of the people she had interviewed.

"I'm going through everything again," she said through gritted teeth. "Even the trash. I must have missed something. I've boiled it down to the groom, his brother, or his best man. But which one, I don't know. I've even got some cop friends in Los Angeles trying to find a connection between Mason Blythe, the brother, and Taylor, since she was down there a lot trying to get into movies. I keep hoping the phone will ring and it'll be them telling me they've found something."

He knew she was really upset because she hadn't bothered to say anything snide to him and had actually given him a straight answer. "I guess the others are being a bit rough on you and Sutter."

Troubled blue eyes met his. He hated seeing her this way. The two of them were so different, so much at odds in almost everything, he knew they could never be more than friends—if that. Still, he liked being around her, and kept finding reasons to see her. Since when had he become such a glutton for punishment?

"Sutter would tell the crime scene unit to open up the space," she murmured, leaning back in her chair, massaging her temples. "He says the case will be solved eventually, and that's that. But I worry that some evidence might be destroyed. The CSI has a few more areas they need to check, mainly the basement. It's a long shot, but nothing else has worked. Still, I feel as if I'm letting everyone down. I'm close to solving the case, I'm sure, but I'm missing something. The killer wasn't a pro, so how was he so clever?"

"You're right," Richie said. "He isn't a pro. And probably

no one went to the wedding planning to kill the bride. But how did they get the murder weapon out of the kitchen without one of the staff noticing?"

"It wasn't in the kitchen. It was in the anteroom on a rolling cart with other used knives and serving utensils. It simply hadn't been moved down to the kitchen yet."

Richie nodded. "So pre-meditation can be pretty definitely ruled out."

"Right."

"Which means the killer wasn't hanging around looking for an opportunity to kill Taylor. Something had to happen that drove him, or her, to it."

She nodded. "The question is: why did the bride go to the anteroom? Answer that, and we should know who the killer is."

She sat upright again, took a sip of the latte, and then picked up a handful of clear plastic evidence bags. They were all filled with odds and ends collected by CSI as they went through the entire facility, including the dumpster and outside trash cans. She fanned the bags across her desk and faced Richie. She looked so beaten down he wanted to pat her shoulder and tell her everything would be all right, but he knew she hated that sort of thing.

"I've looked at this stuff three times already," she said. "I tell myself I missed something but I don't think so."

"What's there?"

She snorted. "Dirty napkins, mostly. A few have names and phone numbers written on them."

"Really?" Richie pulled his chair closer to her so he could

look, too.

"But they all connect to the movie people who seem to have no motive for killing Taylor. I suspect some of them thought about getting together after the wedding, but once the murder happened, it was all they could do to get out of there, and they left the phone numbers behind. Who knows?"

Richie looked over the evidence bags a while, then asked, "What's this?" He lifted a bag containing a piece of paper with a list of names.

"The guest list. The way the paper was cut down, it looks to me like someone, probably the bride or groom, was going to use it as a crib sheet to thank their guests for coming and wanted to make sure they didn't forget anybody."

Richie pointed. "Is that another crib sheet?"

Rebecca reached for the bag he pointed at, then smoothed it on the desktop to better read the typed words under the plastic covering. It was a piece of paper with the word TOAST at the very top, followed by bullet-points. "It was the best man's speech—reminders to him of things to say. It's got a number of nice comments about the bride and groom."

Richie scanned it. "The toast is usually given before the cake cutting and all, so he probably never got a chance to give it."

"He didn't. I asked him."

"He threw it away?"

She nodded. "He said, 'Why should I keep it?'"

Richie read it again. "Weird. It doesn't sound like any best man's speech I've ever heard."

"It's doesn't?"

"Hell, no. Usually, the best man jokes about the groom—he often tells at least one embarrassing story—and then talks about what good friends they are and how lucky the groom is that he actually found a good woman to put up with him. This card has none of that—it's mostly a list of the bride's accomplishments, ending with a few nice words about the groom. This is strange, Rebecca."

She frowned, studying the paper. "I haven't gone to many weddings, but what you describe is the way I remember them."

"The best man actually admitted that he wrote this?" Richie asked.

"All he admitted to was that it was a speech for his toast and that he didn't give it." She pulled the typed guest list side-by-side with the toast speech. "Same paper, same font and font size—but it's typical computer paper, a common font, so that might not mean anything. But still ..."

"Still?" Richie asked.

For the first time that morning he saw a spark of the old Rebecca—the one who was tough, smart, and tenacious. He was glad; he wouldn't want her any other way.

She tapped her finger against her lips as she thought. Very nice lips, in his opinion. He found himself focusing on them until she interrupted the wayward direction of his thoughts by saying, "The best man didn't hide his disdain for the bride, or that he thought Leland was making a big mistake marrying her. It was clear that Taylor didn't like him, and also didn't like him and Leland being so close. The best man even hinted that she had been trying to break up their friendship. It makes no sense he'd sing her praises this way. I need to talk to him again."

Richie smiled at her. "I'd say so."

Just then, Bill Sutter came waltzing into Homicide. "Well, well," he said, eying Richie with a sneer. "Here I was feeling sorry for you, Mayfield, being stuck here all alone on a Saturday morning and thought I'd come in early. Just goes to show ya."

"Glad you're here," Rebecca said. "We need to call in the best man. I've got a few more questions for him, and I think Homicide is the best place to ask them."

Richie stood to leave. "I've got a lot to do this morning, and need to get going. You get this wrapped up by two o'clock, call me. But one way or the other, come to the wedding. Even if not to the church, at least to the reception. I'll text you its location. Most of Homicide will be there, and you should be as well. Please try to make it, Rebecca." Then, something made him add, "For Paavo's sake."

She looked a bit puzzled, but then smiled. He always told her she had a nice smile. He wished he could see it more often. "I will," she said. "Especially if I can manage to get La Belle Maison opened up for them to use. I'm actually feeling a bit optimistic about it."

Chapter 16

Paavo was more nervous than he'd ever been in his life as he waited for the wedding ceremony to begin. He was outdoors in the courtyard at the back of the church, trying to get a little fresh air and sunshine, not to mention having plenty of room to pace.

San Francisco was putting on a show for them—the sky was blue, the temperature mild, and no wind to speak of. It couldn't have been more perfect.

With him were his best man, his partner, Yosh, who was doing all he could to help Paavo keep some slight semblance of calm, and his other groomsmen: Homicide Inspector Luis Calderon, Angie's neighbor Stan Bonnette, her cousin Richie, and Paavo's step-father's good friend Doc Griggs who drove up from Arizona with his new wife, Lupe, to be a part of the wedding.

Paavo's phone buzzed in his pocket. He pulled it out and looked at it.

"Don't answer! You are *not* going out on a call," Yosh said. "I like having my head attached to my body, and Angie would remove it if I allowed you to leave the church grounds even for a minute."

Paavo answered. "Rebecca, what's up?"

He listened without saying a word, and then only said, "Thank you. Thank you so much."

He looked at the others and with a sigh of relief said, "Rebecca caught the murderer. He confessed, and La Belle Maison is open for business."

"Who did it?" Yosh asked.

"The best man. The bride wrote his toast for him and insisted he give it exactly the way she wrote it—filled with praise for her. It was the proverbial straw that broke the camel's back. When he refused, she harangued and threatened him. He said he killed her to spare his best friend a lifetime of misery."

Inspector Calderon chortled. "He only regrets that he has but one bride to get rid of for his friend. Some defense."

"We've got to let Angie and the others know," Paavo said. "I know I'm not supposed to see her before the ceremony, but I guess I can call."

"Let me tell them," Richie suggested. "There are some arrangements that will need to be made. You know her mother had a back-up plan."

"That's right, her secret plan." Paavo had learned that the Amalfis liked to do things their own way, and if Richie wanted to talk it over with them, he wasn't about to interfere. "Okay. Go for it."

ooo

Richie was directed to the room where the bride was getting ready. He knocked on the door, and Bianca opened it.

"You aren't supposed to be here," she hissed.

"I have news about the reception. Big news."

Bianca shut the door on him, and a moment later opened it wide. "Come in."

He actually gulped as he stepped into the most female room he had ever been in. He had visions of what it must have felt like to enter a harem's seraglio. Clothes, particularly under clothes, were strewn about, as was make-up, brushes, curling irons, and something that looked like a clump of curly brown hair on a tabletop. The air was thick with clashing scents of perfume and talc. Angie was already in her bridal gown, and the others were a rose-colored sea of silk and satin. He wanted to flee, but straightened his shoulders and, after a quick glance at Serefina, faced Angie.

He would have taken a deep breath but was afraid he might choke. Then he noticed Micky, the ring bearer, sitting alone in a corner. Micky was the son of Paavo's first partner in Homicide. After Matt Kowalski was killed, Paavo kept in touch with the boy, teaching him to play baseball, basketball, and soccer, taking him to ball games, and just spending time with him. Micky's mother, Katie, at the moment was helping Connie Rogers with her hair.

Richie walked over to Micky and put his hand on the boy's shoulder. "We guys have to stick together," he whispered. Micky smiled up at him and nodded.

Richie faced the women and gave his news. "Rebecca

Mayfield caught Bridezilla's killer. It was the best man. She contacted La Belle Maison, and they'll be able to have the room ready for the reception ... if you want to have it there after all."

The room turned quiet with shock.

"Oh, my God! That's wonderful!" Angie shrieked. Then she realized she was the only one cheering. Her mother, sisters, Connie, and even Richie, looked remarkably crestfallen. "What's going on?" she asked.

"Nothing," Richie said. "I'm only delivering the news."

Angie faced her mother. "I know you made other arrangements. But if it's possible to have the caterer you found go to La Belle Maison, I'm sure the guests wouldn't mind a little delay in the dinner."

Serefina glanced at her other daughters, and then at Angie. "We can manage. We know you want to use that place."

Something about the way her mother said *that place* gave Angie pause. "Wait, you never told me what your other plans were, and I have the feeling all of you rather liked those other plans." Then an almost heretical thought struck her. Her heartbeat quickened. "Are you saying you liked your other plans even more than using La Belle Maison?"

"It's all right," Serefina insisted, then glared at everyone but Angie. "All of us know what you've got your heart set on."

"Oh, for pity's sake. Tell her!" Connie said. "Angie, they came up with a great idea, but they know it isn't the elegant, well-known wedding venue you had your heart set on. But I think you should hear what their plan was before you tell them to change it."

Angie nodded at Connie. "I agree." She faced her mother and sisters. "So, who's going to tell me?"

"All right, I'll do it." Serefina spoke up. "You know we tried to find a replacement for La Belle Maison, and learned all the usual places were taken. But then, I thought we have a great venue right in the family. Richie's club. Big Caesar's has a ballroom, space for a band, liquor, even a kitchen for the food. But it was already taken by a group raising money for Children's Hospital. So, I offered them money. I talked to the guy in charge. For a donation, a big one, he was willing to move his fund-raiser, and came up with a time next month that will actually work better for them. Not that he turned down the donation. I wrote him a check. It's tax deductible, which made your father happy. A little, anyway. And Richie isn't charging us a penny, not even for his staff or his wine."

Angie glanced at Richie. He shrugged and nodded.

"Then," Serefina continued, "we needed food. I don't like catered food all that much, so I called your sisters, relatives, a few friends and explained what happened. All of us spent yesterday and last night cooking our most special recipes for your wedding. So, no, we don't have a fancy caterer, we just have ourselves and our food. We hired a couple more people to help Richie's employees, and we're all set."

Angie's mouth dropped open.

Her oldest sister, Bianca, took over. "This morning, we went to Big Caesar's. Connie was in charge of decorating it in white and rose colors to look like a wedding party should be there. It turned out like something out of Cinderella's ball.

That's how we were going to surprise you. But now, it seems, we don't have to."

By the time she finished talking, Angie had tears in her eyes, and a lump in her throat that was so huge she could scarcely speak. "All of you ... all of you did all that for Paavo and me?"

"We had to have a place to dance at your wedding, Angelina," Serefina said, her head high and her back straight.

"And you offered your club on a Saturday night?" Angie said to Richie, knowing it was biggest night of the week for him.

"I'm happy to be able to help! What more could I do for my favorite"—he glanced at her sisters plus his cousin Gina, mother of the flower girl—"one of my favorite cousins?"

"Thank you so much, Mamma"—Angie hugged Serefina—"and Richie"—she put her arms around her cousin—"and everyone else. Forget the stuffy old La Belle Maison. Whatever was I thinking? We're going Big Caesar's for the best reception this city has ever known."

Chapter 17

Angie's heart was beating so hard she thought she would faint. For the first time, she understood why a bride usually had her father or some other person escort her down the aisle.

The guests had all been seated. She knew Paavo and his grooms had entered from the side door and were waiting at the altar.

Connie made sure Angie's dress and veil looked perfect, and when everyone was in place, she nodded at the church assistant who then opened the church doors and gave the cue to the organist to begin to play.

Angie held her elbows out, grasping the bouquet at her waist. She pushed her shoulders back, lifted her head high, and then placed her right hand on her father's forearm. Salvatore Amalfi, somewhat gaunt due to his heart condition, as tall as Paavo, hawk-nosed, and olive-skinned, smiled at her, beaming encouragement. She didn't think she could move.

She was glad she had chosen Wagner's *Bridal Chorus* as her wedding march. Yes, it was the boring old "Here Comes the Bride," but it was also the song she had imagined hearing on her wedding day from the time she was a little girl. It was the song her mother, her sisters, and her married cousins had all used. As the doors to the church opened, and the first chords began, it filled her heart.

Her mother went first, followed by Bianca, Caterina, Maria, Francesca and then Connie. After her, Micky walked alone, holding a pillow with the rings, and Michaela, the flower girl, trotted behind him strewing rose petals as she went.

Finally, Angie and her father entered the church. She could hear the oohs and aahs from the amazingly large crowd, and saw them surge towards the center aisle as she and Sal slowly moved down it, but most of all she saw Paavo waiting for her. He looked more handsome than she could have imagined in a black tuxedo. She was vaguely aware of his best man and groomsmen behind him, and the priest and deacon standing in front of the altar festooned with flowers. She remembered catching the warmth in some people's eyes as she passed them, and of smiling, but she couldn't have named who she smiled at or who stood nearby.

All she knew was that before long, her father left her side, and Paavo took his place. Connie lifted away her bouquet as she and Paavo listened to the words of the priest.

Everything went as it should. No one stood up to object to the wedding. No cell phone rang, no SWAT team descended on them. Not even a minor earthquake. Nothing horrible happened to ruin the moment.

Somehow, Paavo managed to speak his vows (and didn't, as he'd threatened to do after hearing about one tongue-tied groom, call her his "waffle-wedded wife"), and she said hers, also without flubbing or bursting into tears. Then he lifted back the veil and kissed her. That was when her tears overflowed.

Mendelssohn's *Wedding March*, the most joyous music she had ever heard, shook the rafters and rumbled in her stomach. Connie put her bouquet in her left hand, Paavo took hold of her right, and together the two of them held hands and hurried down the aisle, followed by their attendants.

And so, finally, they were married.

Angie felt her eyes well up again when she entered Richie's nightclub.

Big Caesar's was in the North Beach area, close to Fisherman's Wharf. It was a fun place, popular for its elegant, retro dance club atmosphere with white cloth-covered tables around the dance floor, and where customers wore stylish cocktail dresses, beautifully cut suits, or even tuxedos to dance to swing and jazz music, both fast and slow, written anytime from the 1930's to the present day.

Now, it had been turned into a white wonderland created by Connie and her sisters. She couldn't believe all they'd done, the detail they had gone to with all the banners, napkins, ribbons—and her beautiful wedding cake at center stage.

Angie saw that already most of the guests had found the bar and were availing themselves of the huge offering—beer and most wines free, mixed drinks and premium wines at cost. The guests were an interesting mixture of relatives, family friends, Angie's friends from school, cooking classes, and various jobs she'd had over the years, and lots and lots of police—cops from the precinct where Paavo worked before going to Homicide, and inspectors from different divisions, including CSI. He seemed to have a lot more friends than he thought. Even Medical Examiner Evelyn Ramirez had shown up.

Angie was also glad that people from Paavo's boyhood, not only Doc Griggs, but also Joonas Maki, who had been close friends with Paavo's father, were able to attend. They stood with Aulis Kokkonen talking over old times.

Richie emceed and introduced the wedding party, and then Maria's husband, Dominic Klee and his band played the music for the newlywed's first dance. Angie could find no more appropriate song, after all she and Paavo had been through, than "At Last."

Angie's father stood and thanked all the guests for coming, said a few words about the 'baby' of his family, his youngest, now being a married woman. He gave a blessing, and then the meal was served buffet style. It was an amazing feast of mostly Italian food—manicotti, cannelloni, ravioli, roast pork, lamb, antipasti, stuffed zucchini, and so on—but also with treats from other cuisines as well. Angie had to admit there was more in quantity, variety, and taste than she could have gotten from any caterer in the country. Even her friends from Wings of an Angel had contributed, including Butch's 'special' spaghetti sauce. She hoped he would keep his secret ingredient to himself, or he might be sued by the Italian Benevolent Association.

Best of all, everything had been made with love, which made it all taste even better.

While the food was being served buffet style, Angie saw Rebecca Mayfield enter the club looking prettier than Angie had ever seen her. She wore an emerald green cocktail dress, and her long blond hair softly cascaded down past her shoulders instead of being pulled back in a barrette, while her eyes had been made-up to seem even larger and bluer than usual.

Cousin Richie made a beeline for Rebecca, practically knocking over a young man who had just stepped up to talk to her. Rebecca's eyes lit up when she first saw Richie, although she quickly dropped her gaze as if trying to hide it. Angie smiled to herself as Richie put a possessive hand on Rebecca's waist and escorted her to the bar area. Whatever was going between them, it was not the "nothing" Richie had claimed it was.

Angie wondered if Richie had any inkling of what he was in for if he were to become serious about a homicide inspector—not only her crazy hours and weariness when pursuing a case, but the constant worry he'd have over the danger inherent in her going after murderers.

But then, Angie reminded herself that since Richie's fiancée had been killed, he'd never been serious about any woman. Did he like being around them? Definitely. But serious? Not so much.

Finally, the food was cleared, and the dancing began, starting with the father-daughter dance to *The Way You Look Tonight*. Half way through, they were joined by Paavo and

Serefina, and soon after, Paavo turned Serefina over to Sal, while Angie brought Aulis Kokkonen onto the floor to finish the dance.

Angie couldn't help but remember how, when she first met Paavo, he had to accompany her to a family wedding because she was an eye-witness to a murder and her life was in danger. When the music started, he had asked her to dance. She decided a stiff, homicide detective like him—she'd called him The Great Stoneface back then—wouldn't know how to dance. So then he asked Serefina while she stood there holding up the walls. He'd won Serefina's heart that day, and Angie had learned that he could, in fact, dance very well.

More songs played, and before long, almost everyone was dancing, or drinking, or eating the goodies that remained on the dessert table. As Angie and Paavo circulated to talk to the guests and thank them for coming, she felt good that not only did everyone seem to be having a good time, but they seemed thrilled by the food and location of the reception. She noticed, too, that Richie monopolized Rebecca's time on the dance floor, as well as when she wasn't dancing, and that Rebecca seemed to be enjoying every minute with him.

Angie was talking to Connie when a man she hadn't seen for quite a while came up to them. She had tried hard to find him, and when she succeeded, she sent him a thoughtful and personal invitation. He hadn't sent a response, and she hadn't expected him to show up. But he did. "Max Squire," she said.

Connie spun around, and her face brightened with surprise and something more. Connie had cared about Max, but when they met, he was going through a very difficult time, and nothing ever came of it.

Angie hoped that enough time had passed that he might be ready to look at life anew, to make a fresh start.

"Thank you for coming, Max," Angie said. "I'm sure you and Connie have much to catch up on, so I'll leave you two alone."

He could barely tear his eyes from Connie's but he managed to murmur "Congratulations," to Angie and to thank her for inviting him. He had gone to the wrong location, but a sign was posted on the door directing people here.

Angie nodded, glad to hear it. She found Paavo and pointed out Max. Paavo said "Good," and was about to add something more, when his face froze and he stiffened. "Excuse me," he murmured.

"What is it?" Angie asked, stunned by the sudden change in him. She started to go after him, but then stopped.

The music was an old ballad, *Unforgettable,* and that was what she knew this moment would always be for herself, for Paavo, and for the older woman whose hand he took. He led the woman to the dance floor and put his arm around her. She held herself stiffly even as she put one hand on his shoulder, the other in his. Her skin was well tanned, her hair short and gray. She was tall and trim, and she wore a simple cream-colored dress. Her gaze never wavered from Paavo, and it was filled with pride and love.

Angie watched the two of them dance, and when the song ended, Paavo and the woman walked out of the room.

Probably a few people, not many, noticed the stranger among them. She imagined they assumed the woman was someone Paavo had once helped during one of his cases. They would never know the truth, and she would never tell them. All she knew was that she was thankful her message, sent through Aulis Kokkonen, had somehow reached her, and she had found the strength, and the courage, to come.

Angie was standing alone, thinking about how joyful she felt for Paavo's sake, when Richie grabbed her hand and pulled her to the middle of the dance floor. "Now what?" she asked.

A few people stopped what they were doing to watch. Rebecca Mayfield smiled broadly at them.

Richie took off his jacket and a friend grabbed it. Then he took off his necktie and tossed it to one of Angie's old high school girlfriends standing nearby. She winked and smiled as she caught it.

"Friends," Angie said to their quickly growing audience. "I have not asked him to do a striptease!"

Laughter, hoots, and catcalls sounded.

He unbuttoned the top two buttons of his shirt, then unbuttoned its cuffs.

"Richie, let me remind you, this reception is full of cops!"

More laughter.

He folded back the sleeves of his shirt, nodded at the band and they started playing the *tarantella,* the classic, ageless southern Italian folk music. She, her family, and other relatives always danced it at parties and picnics when she was growing up.

"Come on, Angie, let's show them how it's done," he said, and raised one arm, the other at the small of his back in the traditional stance. She laughed; then, as people clapped in time with the music, with each hand she took a handful of the skirt of her wedding dress, and lifted it slightly from the ground as her feet immediately remembered the jumping two-step. She swished her skirts from side to side as she and Richie twirled round and round in time with the fun, flirtatious song being played. Soon, Richie got his mother to come onto the floor with them, then Serefina, and soon others in the family joined in as well.

Angie used to call the tune "zooma zooma bacala" because the actual Italian words were complicated. Only when she got older and understood what was being said did she realize why everyone would laugh so uproariously when anyone sang those words about the young woman who desperately wanted to get married. She'd tell her mother about each of her suitors, and the mother would have some choice comments about every one of them—starting with the butcher boy and his "meat."

Angie saw Paavo reenter the ballroom alone. He smiled broadly at the sight of her out there dancing with Richie and everyone else. He looked happy. And so was she.

The *tarantella* broke the ice, and before she knew it, other men followed Richie's lead and removed their own jackets and ties, and headed for the dance floor, singing and dancing. Young and old, cops and "civilians" were having fun, and a number of them mixing with each other, which was something that Angie, an acknowledged people-watcher, hadn't expected.

It was soon obvious that some of her girlfriends also had a thing for a guy in a uniform, even if his uniform was currently at home.

The time then came for Yosh to make his toast. Everyone sat, champagne glasses filled and ready, as Paavo's partner stood.

"It's my honor to toast Angie and Paavo on the day of their wedding," Yosh began. "I've been lucky enough to work with Paavo for some time now, and a better, truer partner no one could ask for. He's always had my back, and I've always tried to have his. We all know about his background, how much of a loner he was through most of his life, and how much Aulis Kokkonen meant to him throughout all those years—Aulis was the rock he needed to grow into the man he became. But he was still alone, until one day, he met a very pretty, very rich young woman who someone wanted dead. Paavo managed to keep her alive, and to his—and everyone else's shock—that little bit of a woman managed to save his life as well. As much as he tried to leave her after that, she knew he didn't really want to go, and she didn't want him to, which finally brought them to this happy day. Most best man's toasts have funny stories about the groom, but in our line of work, not much humorous happens—unless you're talking about the time Angie sent Homicide coffee and sandwiches, only the coffee was strawberry flavored, the sandwiches were little heart-shaped things filled with watercress or liver pâté, and nobody wanted to tell Paavo what we thought of his fiancée's taste." Chuckles and groans ensued. "Then, there was also the time she hired a singer to serenade him, but the guy turned up at a crime scene to loudly sing 'O Sole Mio.'" Everyone laughed out loud at that. "It took a long time for Paavo to live that one down." Yosh lifted his glass to the couple, and everyone stood and did the same. "It's been quite a ride, partner. And I know that your life, with Angie—thank God you came to your senses and finally proposed to her—will be even better. Congratulations to you both."

Next, the cake cutting ceremony began with lots of picture-taking, jokes, and well wishes. After the cake was cut, eaten and a few more songs played, Angie's Big Day was almost over. She only had to toss her bouquet, and then she and Paavo would leave the festivities to everyone else as they drove off to start their honeymoon and their life together.

"Are you ready?" Connie asked. Angie had noticed that ever since Max Squire entered the reception, Connie had scarcely left his side, other than to get Stan Bonnette some Tums when he was in pain from having over-eaten.

"I am," Angie said, and Connie handed her the bouquet. Quickly, all the single girls stood in front of her as she went up onto the stage.

She looked over the group, and saw Connie standing at the right-most edge, at the very back. It was going to be a long toss, but she could do it. "Is everyone ready to see who'll be the next bride?" she asked.

As the group roared "Yes!" she turned her back to them, and with a mighty heave, sent her bouquet way up into the air, and then quickly turned around to see if she had aimed correctly.

All the hands were outstretched, and Angie watched in horror as one woman leaped to grab the bouquet as it sailed directly towards Connie. But the woman's timing as well as her catching ability were off, so her hands were still going upward when the bouquet passed overhead, causing her fingertips to hit the flowery missile, making it bounce upward yet again. Connie's face showed her dismay as the treasured orb flew over her head and sailed directly towards, of all people, Cousin Richie.

He looked absolutely horrified as the flying flowers catapulted towards him. He ducked.

Rebecca had been behind him, clearly wanting nothing to do with bouquets or weddings. Out of pure reflex and self-preservation, she tried to take a big step backwards, but in a tight dress and high heels instead of her usual slacks and boots, she wobbled and her arms raised up in an attempt to keep her balance. The bouquet landed snuggly within them.

She stood open mouthed, gaping at it as if it were some mysterious creature from another planet as everyone clapped and cheered.

Richie righted himself, looking every bit as stunned as Rebecca.

The two stared at each other. Rebecca's eyes widened, and then they both did an about-face and hurried off in opposite directions.

As Paavo helped Angie from the stage, they couldn't help but chuckle at the scene that had just played out in front of them and everyone else.

"It's time for us to be on our way," Angie said as she took his arm and leaned close, filled with joy to soon be leaving the reception and to be alone with her new husband. "But something tells me another story is just beginning."

Paavo turned her away from the crowd, so that they only saw each other. "If so, may their days be filled with love and joy the way mine have been from the time we met. I love you, Miss Amalfi, even if I won't be calling you that anymore. And I always will."

She stepped closer to him. "And I love you, Inspector Smith. Forever."

With that, he kissed her—the perfect ending to her perfect Big Day.

The End

From the Kitchen of Angelina Amalfi

ANGIE'S ALMOND BUTTER CAKE WITH CRUNCHY ALMOND TOPPING

If there was ever a dessert recipe you must try, it's this one. Your guests will be sure you bought it in a bakery (and paid a pretty penny for it). Only Angie and you will know how very simple it is to make.

1 & ½ cups sugar (plus 2 teaspoons for topping)

¾ cup (1 & ½ sticks) butter, melted

2 eggs

2 teaspoons almond extract

1 & ½ cups all-purpose flour

¾ cup sliced almonds

Stir 1 & ½ cups sugar and butter in a large bowl. Stir in eggs and almond extract. Blend in flour. Pour in greased 9-inch pan (a spring form pan works especially well). Sprinkle with 2 teaspoons sugar and almonds over top.

Bake at 350 for 40 minutes until golden. Cake may not test clean with a toothpick.

Slice fairly thin—it's rich!

PEACH CLAFOUTIS

6 tablespoons white sugar

1 can sliced peaches

3 eggs

1 & 1/3 cups milk

2/3 cup all-purpose flour

1 & 1/2 teaspoons grated lemon zest

2 teaspoons vanilla

1 pinch salt

½ teaspoon ground cinnamon

2 tablespoons powdered (confectioners) sugar

Optional: vanilla ice cream or whipped cream on top

Preheat oven to 375 degrees. Butter a 10-inch pie pan, and sprinkle 1 tablespoon of sugar over the bottom.

Arrange sliced peaches so that they cover the entire bottom of the pie pan (thick peach slices should be sliced in half). Sprinkle 2 tablespoons of sugar over top of the peaches. Combine the remaining 3 tablespoons of sugar, eggs, milk, flour, lemon zest, cinnamon, vanilla, and salt. Beat until smooth, about 2 minutes. Pour over the fruit in the pan.

Bake for 50 to 60 minutes, until firm and lightly browned. Let stand at least 5 minutes before dusting with confectioners' sugar before serving. Can be served warm or cold.

May be topped with whipped cream or with vanilla ice cream on the side.

FINNISH BLUEBERRY PIE
(since it's hard to find linganberries and they're very tart)
Makes a 9 x 13" pie, serves 12

3/4 cup white sugar
3/4 cup butter, softened
1 teaspoon vanilla
1 egg
1 teaspoon baking powder
2 1/4 cups all-purpose flour
3/8 cup milk
1 pound fresh blueberries
1/2 cup white sugar, or more to taste
Optional: vanilla ice cream or whipped cream

Preheat oven to 400 degrees.

Beat the sugar and the butter until smooth; add vanilla, egg, and baking powder. Stir in flour, 1/2 cup at a time, alternating with a few tablespoons of the milk, until all the flour and milk (use between ¼ and ½ cup) have been incorporated. Dough will be sticky—similar to cookie dough. Spread the dough into the baking dish, with a raised edge of dough around the dish.

Place the blueberries and sugar in a bowl, and lightly mash with a potato masher (it's okay to leave some whole). Spread the blueberry mixture over pie crust in an even layer.

Bake in the preheated oven 15 to 25 minutes, until crust has lightly browned and the filling is thick and bubbling.

Can be serve warm or cold, plain, topped with whipped cream, or with vanilla ice cream on the side.

To hear about new books, please sign up for Joanne Pence's "New Release Mailing List" on her website at www.joannepence.com

The Inspector Rebecca Mayfield Mysteries

Homicide Inspector Rebecca Mayfield, who works with Angie's fiancé Paavo Smith, and Angie's cousin, Richie Amalfi, met and shared their first mystery/adventure in the Christmas novella *The Thirteenth Santa*. Rebecca is a by-the-book detective, who walks the straight and narrow in her work, and in her life. Richie, on the other hand, is a little bit *not* by-the-book. But opposites can and do attract, and there are few mystery two-somes quite as opposite as Rebecca and Richie. Their first full novel adventure takes place in *One O'Clock Hustle*. (The events in *One O'Clock Hustle* occur before the wedding in *Cook's Big Day*.) Here's chapter one:

ONE O'CLOCK HUSTLE

At 1:05 A.M. on Sunday morning, after working twenty-four hours straight on the capture of an armed suspect in the murder of a liquor store clerk, Inspector Rebecca Mayfield sat alone at her desk in Homicide.

She was exhausted. But just as she finished writing up her

notes on the tension-filled arrest, ready to head home for some much-needed sleep, the police dispatcher called: a shooting, one fatality, reported at Big Caesar's Nightclub.

Rebecca had heard of the club, located in San Francisco's touristy North Beach area. She was the first investigator to arrive at the scene, and flashed her badge at the uniformed police officer at the door. "Mayfield. Homicide."

"Good news," Officer Danzig said, all but beaming. "We're holding the killer. The bouncers caught him. He clammed up right away, but you'll find him in the manager's office."

Rebecca's eyebrows rose. She had never had witnesses capture the suspect before. "Interesting. And good; very good." Maybe she would get some sleep tonight after all.

"His name is ..." the officer pulled out his notepad and read from it, "Richard Amalfi."

Rebecca was suddenly jolted wide awake. "What did you say?"

"Richard Amalfi. He's well known at the club, apparently comes here frequently. Everyone calls him Richie."

It can't be. Her mouth went dry. "I see." There are a lot of Amalfis in this city, she told herself. "Did you see him?"

"I did. Not quite six feet, medium build, black hair, late thirties or early forties."

Damn. That sounded like the Richie Amalfi she knew. He was quite a character to be sure, but a murderer? The thought jarred her. She shook her head, needing to focus on the crime, on doing her job. "What do we know about the victim?"

"No name yet. Female, in her thirties, I'd say. We only

know she was a customer. Apparently she came in with the man who killed her."

"Allegedly killed her," Rebecca automatically added.

"Allegedly," Danzig repeated. "Although they said he was caught in the act. The body's in the bookkeeper's office."

Caught in the act ... The words reverberated round and round in her head as she tried to listen to a run-down of the club's layout—the ballroom straight ahead, the coat closet and restrooms to the left, and beyond them, cordoned off with yellow tape, the corridor with the manager's office where Richie was being held, and the bookkeeper's office where the murder took place.

"Was the victim connected to the bookkeeper in some way?" she asked.

"No one has said. The bookkeeper isn't here this time of night."

Rebecca would have been shocked if he was. Nine-to-fivers liked their beauty sleep.

Danzig went on to assure her that he and his partner had immediately shut down the club and no one had been allowed to enter or leave.

She thanked the officer and stepped away from him, drawing a deep breath as she thought of all that was to come.

If Homicide were a family, Richie Amalfi would be a close relative. Rebecca's favorite co-worker, Inspector Paavo Smith, was engaged to Richie's cousin, Angelina Amalfi.

From Paavo, she knew Richie could come up with just about anything that anyone might want. Need something big, small, expensive, cheap, common, or rare? It didn't matter. Cousin Richie could provide. Many people seemed to "know a guy who knows a guy." Well, Richie was that guy—the one people went to when they needed something. She didn't want to get into what that "something" might be, or the legality of how he got it. But that didn't make him a killer ... she hoped.

She entered the elegant ballroom with white cloth-covered tables forming a semi-circle around an empty dance floor. She had never been there before—beer and pizza were her speed; jeans, turtleneck sweaters, black leather jackets, and boots her style.

The popular nightspot had been designed to look like a glamorous nightclub from the forties, the sort of place where Sinatra, Tony Bennett or Dean Martin might have sung, where women dressed in glittery gowns, men wore black or white jackets with bow ties, and "dancing cheek-to-cheek" referred to the couple's faces, not other parts of the anatomy. No hip-hop, rap or, God-forbid, country-western would ever be performed at Big Caesar's.

She could absolutely see Richie in a place like this—as absolutely as she couldn't see him killing anyone. Yet he was "caught in the act," the police officer had said.

As much as she didn't want to believe it, she needed to put aside her personal feelings. She had no more reason to believe he was innocent than she did anyone else accused of a crime. And yet ...

And yet, she couldn't help but remember the day, last Christmas Eve, when she worked alone in Homicide and he came in looking for Paavo for help with a problem. Paavo was off duty, so she ended up helping, and had spent the day and well into the night with him, finally heading home in the early hours of Christmas morning. Their time together hadn't been long, but it had been intense, including chases and shootouts, and the kind of life and death struggles—crazy though they were—that left emotions raw and defenses down. To her amazement, she had enjoyed being with him.

She then used the next several days wondering if she'd been stupid to have spent so much time with him.

Not that anything had "happened" between them. Heaven forbid! After all, from the moment she first met him, she knew he wasn't her type, and he clearly realized the same about her. Still, from time to time, she couldn't help but wonder ...

In any case, he never contacted her again—which told her that the only thing stupid was to have wasted any time whatsoever thinking about him. Of course, if he had called and asked her out, she would have refused to go. She wondered if he hadn't realized that. He was, she had discovered, curiously perceptive.

The band now jauntily played *"The Best is Yet to Come,"* but a sullen, wary mood blanketed the room.

When she left the ballroom, she found that her partner, Bill Sutter, had arrived. He was taking statements from the bouncers. Rebecca walked around to get a quick feel for the nightclub's layout and exits, both doors and windows.

Despite wanting to see and question Richie, she would save him for last.

From her several years of experience in Homicide, she knew that the more she learned about a situation the better her first questions would be, and the better she could judge the veracity of a suspect's answers. Since she knew the alleged "perp," she was going to have to be even more by-the-book in this case than she normally was.

She ducked under the yellow crime scene tape. A cop stood at the door of one of the offices.

"Homicide," Rebecca said as she put on latex gloves and entered the office. The victim lay face up in the center of the room.

She appeared to be in her early thirties and to Rebecca's eye the sort of blonde—beautiful, slim, and expensively dressed—that fit easily in a classy place like Big Caesar's; the sort of woman she could imagine Richie going out with.

A gunshot had struck her heart. Death was most likely instantaneous or close to it. Blood soaked the carpet beneath her.

Rebecca surveyed the rest of the room. The window was open wide, bringing in blustery, cold air. Piles of papers lay in a wind-tossed jumble across the desk where a brass nameplate read "Daniel Pasternak." Behind it hung a sappy Thomas Kincaid painting of little sparkling pastel-colored cottages ready-made for Disney's seven dwarfs. On the floor near the body lay a small satin handbag.

Rebecca picked it up and opened it. The bag was empty except for two twenties and a lipstick. No cell phone; no credit cards. That was surprising, and odd.

Just then, the medical examiner, Evelyn Ramirez, arrived. She wore a red sequined blouse, black silk slacks, and diamonds. Her black hair was pulled back tight and pinned up in a sleek chignon. She had obviously been called away from some big shindig and intended to return to it soon.

The M.E. quickly took in the body and its surroundings. "Well, this'll be fast."

Rebecca watched Ramirez do the preliminary examination to make sure no big surprises turned up—such as the corpse had actually been dead for twelve hours before someone found her, not twenty seconds like everyone said. The entry wound indicated the shot had been fired at close range, a few feet away, which was consistent with the killer and victim being together in the room.

With the exam concluded, the time had come for Rebecca to face Richie.

She took a deep breath and opened the door to the office of the nightclub manager.

Richie stood at the window, his back to her, looking into the night. His wrists were handcuffed behind him.

Two cops sat near the desk—a desk overflowing with paperwork. When Rebecca entered, they walked over to the door and stood beside it.

Richie slowly turned and faced her. Even in handcuffs he seemed calm, cool, and suave in a black jacket, white shirt, and black bow tie, almost like something out of a James Bond movie. Or, more in keeping with him and his friends, *The Godfather.*

"Richie Amalfi," she whispered.

He took a step towards her, then stopped, his deep-set, heavy-lidded brown eyes troubled and questioning. As he gazed at her, she saw something else in them, but she wasn't sure what.

She steeled herself and raised her head high, giving him a cold, icy stare.

His shoulders seemed to sag at that. "Rebecca Rulebook," he murmured, then pushed a noisy breath past his lips, and wryly shook his head. "Guess I should kiss my ass good-bye."

His saying that, his thinking that way about her, momentarily stung, but she pushed the feelings aside and concentrated on the job before her. She pulled out a chair for Richie, and then another for herself facing it. Truth be told, she moved the furniture around to give herself time to think, and to give her breathing a chance to return to normal.

"Have a seat, Richie." She prided herself on being a cop. Raised in Idaho, she had always followed the straight and narrow, and believed that all God's children were created equally. But if one of them got out of line, the full power of the law should stomp down until they saw the light. And Richie Amalfi was no exception.

"Look, Rebecca—"

"Inspector Mayfield," she said harshly, too harshly. She sat in the chair she had provided for herself and waited. She knew the rumors that he was "connected." She hadn't wanted to believe there was anything bad about him, but if he did kill someone in her city, on her watch, she didn't give a damn about those connections or family ties—current or future.

He sat facing her. "I didn't kill Meaghan Blakely." He leaned towards her as he spoke, his gaze intense, his voice earnest. "I found her body, that's all."

Thank you, she thought. He had just identified the victim. She ignored his protestation of innocence. All suspects did that.

"Tell me about Meaghan Blakely. Where does she live?"

"I don't know. I just met her." He started to stand, then changed his mind and remained seated. She could sense his tension, his need to fidget—he constantly fidgeted that one day they spent together. It drove her crazy.

Just then, Bill Sutter walked into the room.

Rebecca's partner was a burden to her. She knew from watching the other homicide inspectors that loyalty to one's partner was important, so she never complained no matter how furious he made her.

"Never-Take-A-Chance" Sutter was in his late fifties, about six feet tall, slim, with short steel gray hair, a long face, multiple bags under watery gray eyes, and thin, constantly down-turned colorless lips. He had been in Homicide so long he could have doubled as a walking, talking history book. Unfortunately, he had lost interest in the job and focused more on his retirement than his day-to-day duties. He talked about it all the time, and obsessed with worry that, like a character in a movie he once saw, he might be killed in the line of duty before his retirement day arrived. As a result, he did all he could to avoid putting himself in any danger—a difficult task when confronting killers.

Richie and Sutter eyed each other warily. Richie stiffened.

"Please continue," Rebecca said.

Squaring his shoulders as best he could with his hands cuffed, Richie stated, "I'm not saying another word until I talk to my lawyer!"

Sutter folded his arms and with a scowl faced Rebecca. "As far as I'm concerned, that does it for him. He wants to lawyer up, fine. I've got two witnesses' statements that he held the murder weapon and was trying to escape out the window when they caught him. I say we take him down to the station. If we can't question him, we book him."

A part of her wanted to believe Richie was innocent, but the evidence told her otherwise and she was too tired to try to argue against it, especially since Richie had no interest in cooperating. "You're right," she said finally.

Sutter nodded. "Good. Look, I'll handle everything. Go home, get some sleep. We've been at work non-stop since yesterday afternoon. We'll have clearer heads tomorrow."

At Sutter's mention of sleep, all the fatigue she had tried to ignore struck and the quiet throbbing of her head became an insistent drumbeat. She nodded. Without allowing herself to look back at Richie one last time, sick at heart, she left the room.

Continue with *One O'Clock Hustle* wherever ebooks and print books are sold.

About the Author

Joanne Pence was born and raised in northern California. She has been an award-winning, USA Today best-selling author of mysteries for many years, but she has also written historical fiction, contemporary romance, romantic suspense, a fantasy, and supernatural suspense. All of her books are now available as e-books, and most are also in print.

Joanne hopes you'll enjoy her books, which present a variety of times, places, and reading experiences, from mysterious to thrilling, emotional to lightly humorous, as well as powerful tales of times long past.

Visit her at http://www.joannepence.com. Also, to hear about new books, please sign up for Joanne's New Release Mailing List.

The Inspector Rebecca Mayfield Mysteries

Readers enjoyed the interaction between Homicide Inspector Rebecca Mayfield, who works with Angie's fiancé Paavo Smith, and Angie's cousin, Richie Amalfi, in the Christmas novella, *The Thirteenth Santa,* and asked for more! Rebecca is a by-the-book detective, who walks the straight and narrow in her work, and in her life. Richie, on the other hand, is not at all by-the-book. But opposites can and do attract, and there are few mystery two-somes quite as opposite as Rebecca and Richie.

ONE O'CLOCK HUSTLE

TWO O'CLOCK HEIST

THREE O'CLOCK SÉANCE

Plus a Christmas Novella: The Thirteenth Santa

The Angie Amalfi Mysteries

Gourmet cook, sometime food columnist, sometime restaurant critic, and generally "underemployed" person Angelina Amalfi burst upon the mystery scene in SOMETHING'S COOKING, in which she met San Francisco Homicide Inspector Paavo Smith. Since that time she's wanted two things in life, a good job...and Paavo.

Here are the Angie mysteries in the order written:
SOMETHING'S COOKING
TOO MANY COOKS
COOKING UP TROUBLE
COOKING MOST DEADLY
COOK'S NIGHT OUT
COOKS OVERBOARD
A COOK IN TIME
TO CATCH A COOK
BELL, COOK, AND CANDLE
IF COOKS COULD KILL
TWO COOKS A-KILLING
COURTING DISASTER
RED HOT MURDER
THE DA VINCI COOK
COOKING SPIRITS

Plus a Christmas novella: Cook's Curious Christmas (The novella is also available in COOK'S CHRISTMAS CAPERS along with the Inspector Rebecca Mayfield novella, The Thirteenth Santa.)

Supernatural Suspense

Ancient Echoes

Top Idaho Fiction Book Award Winner

Over two hundred years ago, a covert expedition shadowing Lewis and Clark disappeared in the wilderness of Central Idaho. Now, seven anthropology students and their professor vanish in the same area. The key to finding them lies in an ancient secret, one that men throughout history have sought to unveil.

Michael Rempart is a brilliant archeologist with a colorful and controversial career, but he is plagued by a sense of the supernatural and a spiritual intuitiveness. Joining Michael are a CIA consultant on paranormal phenomena, a washed-up local sheriff, and a former scholar of Egyptology. All must overcome their personal demons as they attempt to save the students and learn the expedition's terrible secret....

Ancient Shadows

One by one, a horror film director, a judge, and a newspaper publisher meet brutal deaths. A link exists between them, and the deaths have only begun ....

Archeologist Michael Rempart finds himself pitted against ancient demons and modern conspirators when a dying priest gives him a powerful artifact--a pearl said to have granted Genghis Khan the power, eight centuries ago, to lead his Mongol warriors across the steppes to the gates of Vienna.

The artifact has set off centuries of war and destruction as it conjures demons to play upon men's strongest ambitions and cruelest desires. Michael realizes the so-called pearl is a philosopher's stone, the prime agent of alchemy. As much as he would like to ignore the artifact, when he sees horrific deaths and experiences, first-hand, diabolical possession and affliction, he has no choice but to act, to follow a path along the Old Silk Road to a land that time forgot, and to somehow find a place that may no longer exist in the world as he knows it.

Historical, Contemporary & Fantasy Romance

Dance with a Gunfighter

Willa Cather Literary Award finalist for Best Historical Novel.

Gabriella Devere wants vengeance. She grows up quickly when she witnesses the murder of her family by a gang of outlaws, and vows to make them pay for their crime. When the law won't help her, she takes matters into her own hands.

Jess McLowry left his war-torn Southern home to head West, where he hired out his gun. When he learns what happened to Gabriella's family, and what she plans, he knows a young woman like her will have no chance against the outlaws, and vows to save her the way he couldn't save his own family.

But the price of vengeance is high and Gabriella's willingness to sacrifice everything ultimately leads to the book's deadly and startling conclusion.

The Dragon's Lady

Against the background of San Francisco at the time of the Great Earthquake and Fire of 1906 comes a tale of love and loss. Ruth Greer, wealthy daughter of a shipping magnate, finds a young boy who has run away from his home in Chinatown— an area of gambling parlors, opium dens, sing-song girls, as well as families trying to eke out a living. It is also home to a number of highbinder tongs, the infamous "hatchet men" of Chinese lore.

There, Ruth meets the boy's father, Li Han-lin, the handsome, enigmatic leader of one such tong, and discovers he is neither as frightening, cruel, or wanton as reputation would have her believe. As Ruth's fascination with the area grows, she finds herself pulled deeper into the intrigue of the lawless area, and Han-lin's life. But the two are from completely different worlds, and when both worlds are shattered by the earthquake and fire that destroys San Francisco, they face their ultimate test.

Seems Like Old Times

When Lee Reynolds, nationally known television news anchor, returns to the small town where she was born to sell her now-vacant childhood home, little does she expect to find that her first love has moved back to town. Nor does she expect that her feelings for him are still so strong.

Tony Santos had been a major league baseball player, but now finds his days of glory gone. He's gone back home to raise his young son as a single dad.

Both Tony and Lee have changed a lot. Yet, being with him, she finds that in her heart, it seems like old times...

The Ghost of Squire House

For decades, the home built by reclusive artist, Paul Squire, has stood empty on a windswept cliff overlooking the ocean. Those who attempted to live in the home soon fled in terror. Jennifer Barrett knows nothing of the history of the house she inherited. All she knows is she's glad for the chance to make a new life for herself.

It's Paul Squire's duty to rid his home of intruders, but something about this latest newcomer's vulnerable status...and resemblance of someone from his past...dulls his resolve. Jennifer would like to find a real flesh-and-blood man to liven her days and nights--someone to share her life with—but living in the artist's house, studying his paintings, she is surprised at how close she feels to him.

A compelling, prickly ghost with a tortured, guilt-ridden past, and a lonely heroine determined to start fresh, find themselves in a battle of wills and emotion in this ghostly fantasy of love, time, and chance.

Dangerous Journey

C.J. Perkins is trying to find her brother who went missing while on a Peace Corps assignment in Asia. All she knows is that the disappearance has something to do with a "White Dragon." Darius Kane, adventurer and bounty hunter, seems to be her only hope, and she practically shanghais him into helping her.

With a touch of the romantic adventure film *Romancing the Stone*, C.J. and Darius follow a trail that takes them through the narrow streets of Hong Kong, the backrooms of San Francisco's Chinatown, and the wild jungles of Borneo as they pursue both her brother and the White Dragon. The closer C.J. gets to them, the more danger she finds herself in—and it's not just danger of losing her life, but also of losing her heart.

[This is a completely revised edition of novel previously published as *Armed and Dangerous*.]

ooo

Look for the books by Joanne Pence by visiting her website at http://www.joannepence.com, and learn about new books by signing up for her New Release Mailing List.

CPSIA information can be obtained at www.ICGtesting.com
Printed in the USA
LVOW07s0310171016

509054LV00001B/75/P